# About the Author

Amanda Aubrey-Burden is Welsh born and bred and has lived all over Wales and knows its myths and legends well. She has always had a deep interest in the paranormal and has had personal experience of what can happen when you dabble in the dark side…

# Dedication

*I dedicate this book to all of my friends and family who have kept the faith, and in me, and for all the lost souls who feel they have no place in this world; know that if you don't find it in this one, you will in the next; Love always finds a way.*

My husband, Nigel, for allowing me the time and the space to make it happen and also the means with a new laptop!

Good friend Lindsay Forrest-Gouveia for her unstinting support from start to finish!

Tim Lyn for giving me the confidence to take the devil by the horns and just do it!

Debbie Pritchard for her encouragement and for having faith in my ability when I did not.

And last, but not least, two of the characters in the book, Cerys and Jonas who came to me in a dream one night after I'd thrown in the towel and persuaded me to carry on. It is probably due to these two more than anyone that the book was completed.

Amanda Aubrey-Burden

# Devil's Messiah

Austin Macauley
PUBLISHERS LTD.

Copyright © Amanda Aubrey-Burden (2016)

The right of Amanda Aubrey-Burden to be identified as author of this work has been asserted by her in accordance with section 77 and 78 of the Copyright, Designs and Patents Act 1988.

All rights reserved. No part of this publication may be reproduced, stored in a retrieval system, or transmitted in any form or by any means, electronic, mechanical, photocopying, recording, or otherwise, without the prior permission of the publishers.

Any person who commits any unauthorized act in relation to this publication may be liable to criminal prosecution and civil claims for damages.

A CIP catalogue record for this title is available from the British Library.

ISBN 9781786935137 (Paperback)
ISBN 9781786935144 (E-Book)

www.austinmacauley.com

First Published (2016)
Austin Macauley Publishers Ltd.
25 Canada Square
Canary Wharf
London
E14 5LQ

# Chapter 1

The moaning stops at the first crack of stone. Turning their dark and wearisome eyes towards the great altar, the lost souls who live out their purgatory in the old abandoned church watch uncertainly as the great split of rock now widens as something big and powerful pushes up from beneath. With an intense grating sound of complaint, the two slabs of stone began to rise and part from each other gradually coming to rest at an angle. Something dark moves between them and the spirits ease back into the shadows their disquiet now replaced by an unfathomable fear.

The creature that emerges from the fine mist of dust is not a being they have ever encountered before. Indeed, she would look strange to any eye, for she is of two worlds. But it has been a long time since she walked in this one and she doesn't come alone. For with her are two huge wraiths of the deepest black; they are thickly set and emanate bridled menace.

The creature, in contrast, is tall and willowy-slim and possessed of features much more defined, and as she steps forward into the faint light cast by the window of stained glass, we see a finely chiseled face that you could say was neither plain nor beautiful. But the features have a hidden, mystical quality as the eyes glow fiercely; one minute a bright blazing white the next, a feverish red. The mane of silvery hair falls well below her waist and ripples constantly as though alive about her head, and the simple robe that hugs the long frame pulsates gently as colours chase themselves around forever trapped within the fiendish fabric.

She turns her terrible gaze upon the spirits who seek to hide themselves away in dark corners, and in a voice that is surprisingly as melodious as it is gravelly and unearthly, she calls out and summons them to her. And they, like the sailors of old driven mad by the songs of the Sirens, could no more resist than if the very Devil had called them himself, and cringing and wailing they prostrate themselves before her and at the sight of their complete and hopeless subjugation, the eyes turn black and she laughs softly.

"Oh you poor, lost children of the night! How long has it been for your sufferance in this plight? The endless wait, the agony of woe, the veil that has trapped and tormented you through the ages. But not for much longer, I can promise you that."

With pale fingers she beckons them forward and they rise, weak in compliance, huddling in their misery, "Why, come, my darlings, and cease your whining. Come closer still for I would share with you such tidings as to lift your sore and sorry hearts and break forever the binds that hold you fast. But first."

The lips part in a parody of a smile, and as the lost souls' moan and wait to hear their fate, a light suddenly blooms at the far end of the church and the creature, caught completely by surprise, narrows her eyes and they flare a dull orange as her words hang in the air like an unseen ghost.

The ball of light grows bigger and brighter as it throws off the shadows and sensing some imminent change in the atmosphere the spirits slowly turn to face the brilliance and then crumple down to the ground as though struck by a mighty hand. They coil and curl tightly upon themselves, for they know of this light and what dwells within it but the creature lifts one well-arched eyebrow and waits.

The first figure to emerge from the light is also tall and willowy, but her carriage is regal and graceful and beautifully bright. Shimmering robes of the purest white fold and unfold about her, and showing just slightly over the tops of her shoulders are the silvery feathers of the tiniest wings. Her flowing hair, that has the look of the finest spun gold, frames a softly featured but determined face, and the eyes, of the most striking and delicate cornflower blue, look back steadily at the creature as she makes her approach. More figures glide forward until there are seven of them arranged and positioned in the formation of an arrow.

They are, all of the same as to be almost identical, and emanate the same single-minded intensity of purpose. The lead figure raises a hand and they glide to a halt just feet short of the souls who lie silent and unmoving at the foot of the steps.

"I am Lorelius, guardian of this church; head of the Holy Sisters and appointed by those highest in the Heavenly Realm to protect this house of God, and *you*,

you foul creature, have dared to breach the most sacred of all portals and permeate the sanctity therein!"

Her voice is strong, strident, thrumming with an undercurrent of power that warns against defiance with the assurance of swift and merciless retribution.

"How dare you!"

The church reverberates at the thunder in her words. And as though convulsed with shame, the lost souls emit one long wail before returning to silence, a writhing mass of long-held misery. Their offering is ignored as Light and Darkness lock gazes with each other and energies as strange as they are ancient start to build up around them like a gathering storm.

"Oh I dare, alright..." drawled the Creature, "I have taken possession of this..."

She flicks a hand contemptuously, "Place! As I have these... how shall we call them? Pilgrims...? Petitioners...? No...prisoners...yes! Prisoners of Purgatory! Much more apt, don't you agree?"

"Don't you mock me! Don't you *dare* bandy words with me whilst you seek to distract and disguise your true intent! You have not broken through from the pits of hell for the sake of these souls and their salvation! I have met your kind before and a fallen angel you *are not*! We will cast you back and we will cast you down deep!" said the angel called Lorelius, "For we will not suffer you, nor the devil beasts you have brought with you on hallowed ground a moment longer!"

She rises at speed in a blaze of brilliant white, and with an audible whoosh the rest of the Sisterhood ascends with her. Lorelius sweeps her arm down and points at the fractured altar with an outrage that resonates throughout the host, and their fury blazes further as they see the extent of the sacrilege that has been wrought.

The Creature observes their distress with an impassive air but the lost souls cringe and the giant henchmen that guard the breach shift momentarily but stay at their posts. Lorelius suddenly swoops down so that she's just inches from the face of the Creature. In a quiet voice, all the more dreadful for its intensity, the angel's eyes blaze blue fire as she intones deliberately,

"You have defiled my Father's church; you have forced entry through the most sacred part of his house, and you have broken every law there is of God's jurisdiction! And in his name…IN GOD'S HOLY NAME!" she thunders and in a flash she is back up among the Sisters, "AND ALL THE ARCH-ANGELS…"

Collectively they begin to spin, swirling funnels of incredible light and as they pick up speed they whirl even faster as the air crackles madly and the long white hair of the Creature snakes out and begins to frizzle.

"AS THE GUARDIANS OF THE GATEWAY AND THE POWER VESTED IN US, WE BANISH YOU FROM THIS SACRED PLACE AND COMM-AND YOUR RETURN TO THE REALMS OF HELL! BACK TO THE DEPTHS! DOWN TO THE PIT! WE

CAST YOU BACK! WE CAST YOU DOWN! IN THE NAME OF THE FATHER, THE SON, AND THE HOLY SPIRIT, WE COMMAND YOU NOW, WE COMMAND YOU FROM OUR SIGHT!"

With an abrupt flourish the Holy Sisters whirl to a sudden halt each arm extended stiffly out and stretched to a point. The air remains charged and the radiance about them all but sears the naked eye, but the Creature, she flinches not, nor does she shade the devilish eyes that have now turned an opaque black. She stares back at the hovering host as slowly her simmering mane of white loses all life and animation and becomes motionless. Silence descends as the lost souls cease in their lamentations and a heavy stillness pervades the air Lorelius looks at the Creature and the Wraiths that still remain and a frown wrinkles the alabaster brow. Feeling the eyes of the other angels on her, she also hears their thoughts. There is a frisson of confusion along the usual calm channels, and as she calls for order the light that surrounds them seems to falter and weaken but she harnesses their disquiet and signals they follow her lead. Like wilting flowers, they descend slowly before the baleful glare of the figure below, and they alight before the Creature who observes their shocked gazes and gives a small smirk.

"Tut, tut, tut, oh my, oh my..."

The eyes have returned to insectile scarlet, smoldering with spite, "What are you going to do now? It seems to be that you're powerless here, indeed I would even go so far as to say you've been... *abandoned!*"

She shouts the last word and throws back her awful head and emits a strange barking sound; her hair comes back to life and ripples wildly and lightning fast, she leers in at them and waggles her tongue obscenely. The Sisterhood recoil and a slight fluttering of their wings denote a barely-checked panic.

"Stand back, you foul being!" Lorelius cries in sudden fury.

Bewilderment runs through her and it is all she can do to hold the host in check. Something has gone wrong, terribly wrong! And as she reaches out beyond the babble of her sisters for succour and heavenly guidance there is nothing but an endless void but she rallies herself for the sake of the sisters holding fast to her innate strength and unshakeable faith.

"What have you done? What evil is this! What deeds have you unleashed so dark as to attack the sanctity of my Father's power and in His own house!"

"His house! *His house?*" taunts the Creature, "Oh my dear, you are as mistaken as your role here now is redundant for it is *my* house now so concern yourself not! But, I will tell you this..." she leans forward, her thin face taking on a wolfish look.

"The wants of the world are changing; dark doings and deep desires have been creeping across the earth like a slow disease and my father would be neglectful – indeed he would be *failing* in his duty were he to ignore the signs and not reach out and seize the day! And where have you been? And what have you and your holy hierarchy done about it? Hmm now let me see... ah, nothing, I believe! But please, feel at liberty to correct me if I'm wrong…?"

Again the raised eyebrow of contempt.

"You have been complacent, have you not? So certain beyond question that earthly equilibrium had been maintained … so convinced, so self-assured, so … safe, that your eyes became your enemy and they looked the other way! Therefore, *we* are now reaping the rewards of *our* attention and the lack of yours thereof, and know that the taking of this church is just the beginning…"

With a chill that stirs the feathered wings, the Sisterhood immediately comprehend and as one they experience an emotion hitherto unknown to them that is shame.

"What is your name … who are you?" asks Lorelius haughtily.

"My name? Who am I?" the Creature echoes mockingly, "I will give you my name since you gave me yours. But who I am, or what I was, matters not! My name is Selinus and now you have far outstayed your welcome, in fact, forgive me *not!* But I would go as far as to say you're trespassing…"

Suddenly she raises her voice, "LOST SOULS OF THIS PLACE, I CALL ON YOU TO RISE UP AND STAND WITH ME NOW!"

The Holy Sisters step back in surprise as the roiling black mass surge fluidly to their feet and face Selinus with avid expectation. The Creature spreads her white hands in appeal and coos lovingly at her rapt audience as the angels look on helplessly.

"It is time, children, it is now your time to pledge your allegiance and shake off the godly shackles that have held you here. Come to me; give yourself willingly to us, and you will never know such misery again nor endure the endless punishment of..."

"Evil creature, cease your blasphemy! You go too far! You have *no right!*" Selinus turns swiftly on Lorelius and bares her teeth like a wild beast.

"Seek *not*, to lecture me!" she snarls. "Dare *not*, to even think of thwarting *me!* You have had your chance with this miserable lot for over three hundred years and now it is too late! So cease your prating, your power is waning, sister, and you have no influence here! For believe me when I tell you, I will have them for my own – each and every one of them! And there's nothing, *nothing,* you can do!"

"But they are not yours to take! Release your hold and let them be – your fight is not with them."

"But I will have them nevertheless. We have a history you see..." says the Creature enigmatically. Her voice rises again like a terrible wind and the angels flinch before it.

"LOST SOULS! LOST CHILDREN OF THE NIGHT! GIVE YOURSELVES TO ME AND MAKE THE FINAL PLEDGE! A NEW DAY IS COMING – A NEW DAWN IS WAKING! DECIDE YOUR FATE NOW AND FREEDOM WILL BE YOURS – BOW DOWN TO ME AND I WILL RELEASE YOU!"

"NO! You cannot!" Lorelius cries but further words die in her throat as with an alacrity borne of supernatural speed the lost souls swoop down before turning about face.

They stand silently before her in a rigid line. Previously and like all souls sentenced to purgatory, these kinds of spirits are featureless and faceless, drifting aimlessly forever like random wisps of black smoke. But there is structure and substance about them now and more worrying still, an aura of fervent anticipation.

As Selinus squawks in triumph, the angels shudder and then sigh in collective sadness. Moving forwards Lorelius appeals to the dark forms in one last desperate attempt to divert them from their intent.

"Don't do this. It's not too late. Stop now and step back, for if you stand against us and the power of God, you will forfeit any chance of salvation and truly will be lost forever."

The gentleness of her words falls on ears past caring, and knowing the truth of this she moves back and steels herself for the attack she knows is coming. Silently and with great calmness there passes among the angels the understanding that, for them, their Armageddon had come. And, stilled by a serene acceptance of their fate, they reach out with love and words of encouragement to each other.

"It will be a fair fight, you cannot argue with that ... you'll lose, of course, but at least you're evenly matched and that must give you some hope, albeit a false one!"

The Creature's enjoyment of the moment is marred by the angels' air of peaceful resignation and she throws them a sharp scowl, "You'll not look so fine and full of holy grace once they've finished with *you!* They've got a few old scores to settle, you can be sure of that! And once you've been dragged down to the deepest pit, there will await you such torments as you can never imagine, and then, when..."

Her words are cut short as a great white fist of light punches through the darkened church and with it comes the sound of a strident horn that reverberates loudly around the walls and up to the roof.

"Father!"

The Holy Sisters cry as one and all are filled with a great joy as the light pulsates and the horn blasts and the radiance surrounds them as one by one they are drawn lovingly back towards its core. The dark souls drop to the floor and turn away shielding their eyes as the Creature shrieks with fury. Eyes blazing, she paces and rants as her hair whips and snaps and a rumbling from deep below tells her that a moment has been missed and this fuels her anger as she screams across the divide,

"That's it, flee to your God and don't come back! And if you dare step foot in here again, I will rip the wings from your back myself! Do you hear me! Do you HEAR ME?"

As Lorelius is the last angel to be gathered into the light she hears the tirade. But the radiance is soothing and her relief so great, she cares not. Saved from the fires of hell by the very hand of God Himself, she only has room for gratitude and love.

But just before the light envelopes her completely, she looks out to the Creature and catches her eye and knows in that instant that the challenge will be met…

# Chapter 2

Nobody knows it yet, but it is the last day of what had been a glorious summer. Beyond the dazzling azure of dreamy blue skies, dark clouds gather on the horizon but the imminent change in the weather is barely noticed by the young woman as she walks along the road. In her hands she holds a mobile phone that takes up all of her attention.

She's brassy-looking for someone so young, not yet out of her late teens but not unattractive. Dressed skimpily and in the latest fashions, her face is heavy with cosmetics that make her look older than what she is. And her hair, sleeked back in a bob is vibrantly red with blonde highlights feathering the fringe. She cuts a striking figure, but there is an air of petulance about the bottom lip and she frowns suddenly as she hears a familiar voice.

"Delyth! *Del!* Wait up!"

She slows to a stop and assumes a stance that can only be described as stroppy.

*"What!"*

It is a statement not a question and suggests that the intrusion is greatly resented. Another young woman of about the same age comes running into view and is in stark contrast to Delyth, with a more natural and less cultivated look. Her chestnut hair is long and rippling, her face sun kissed and pretty with wide, hazel eyes. She wears a long summer dress with pale pastel prints, and as she catches up there's an air of mild annoyance about her that is reflected in the pink cheeks.

"Is your phone not working, then? *Again!*" she says pointedly, "Del, your mam is going spare trying to get hold of you – ended up sending me instead, like I haven't got better things to do! So best you ring her – or better still I'd go back if I were you."

Delyth tuts her disgust and gives a defiant toss of her head.

"Well you're not *me,* are you, Cerys! And what are you now – my keeper? Just because my mam married your da doesn't make you anything other than my stepsister and you're certainly no better than me, so if I want your advice, I'll ask for it; alright?"

Cerys rolls her eyes and emits a long-suffering sigh. Having a stepsister was hard enough, but when there was only a year between them, with Cerys being the eldest, the jostling for position was a constant battle. Even after two years it was a relentless fight and remarks like this were all too common. But she went with it as best she could, believing that it was her place, as the eldest to lead by example. And besides, the happiness of her father was involved in all of this; they had gone through a lot together since losing mam and she loved him more than life itself.

"Okay, okay, I was just passing on the message so get off your high-horse, Delyth. Your mam isn't a woman to argue with when she gets going, but she wants you back at the house *now*, so it's up to you, just don't shoot the messenger!"

"So what does she want now? Or rather more accurately, what have *I* done wrong now! I'm not in trouble, am I...?" Delyth pouts uncertainly and Cerys softens.

The older girl is by nature a positive spirit and loath to hold a grudge. It is a beautiful morning, it's Saturday, and she'd had a letter that morning confirming her place at college. All the years of study and exams had been worth it. Her dream of becoming a nurse was now underway, and as she looks at Delyth still trapped in the midst of teenage angst she almost feels sorry for her. Too young to sign on the dole, and reluctant to do anything other than hang around with like-minded friends and moan, Delyth had no life-aspirations other than having a good time when she could get it and dreaming the impossible.

"She said something about not doing your jobs, you know, like tidying your bedroom and stuff, just the usual. Where were you going anyway?" Cerys adds out of curiosity.

"Town!" says Delyth flatly. "Where else is there if you want to get out of this dump! Nothing ever happens here, I could die of boredom! Not that it matters now you've found me. I'll have to go back now! Five more minutes and I could've been on the bus!"

She glowers at Cerys from beneath her fringe, "Not that I wanted to come and live here in the first place! Your dad's alright, I suppose, he takes care of us, the house is nice and we don't struggle anymore; it's just a shame I've got a hippy for a half-sister, but hey-ho, I guess you can't have everything!"

Cerys shrugs her shoulders; she's heard it all before and worse.

"We could try being friends, you know, Delyth… there's no law that says you've got to be so nasty all the time! You'll soon be eighteen, isn't it time you stopped acting like a spoilt brat and grew up?"

Delyth pouts some more, "It's alright for *you*! You've passed your exams and have something to look forward to. What have I got trapped in this dump! All of my friends, my *proper* friends are miles away in Swansea, my mam's too busy looking after *your* da to pay much attention these days, *and*, there are no decent blokes around here worth a snog; all they want to do is get you drunk and pregnant! It's all so unfair!" Cerys had to bite her lip to stop the laughter bubbling up, Delyth could be so dramatic at times

"Oh Del, give it a rest, please, you'll have me crying in a minute!"

Delyth drew herself up with as much dignity as she could muster.

"Yeah, that's right, have a *laugh*! Who do you think you are, anyway, Cerys? Laura bloody Ashley with your flowery dresses and your squeaky clean face always smiling like an idiot! Anyway, I'm not speaking to you,

you've ruined my day now anyway, so you can bloody well–"

She breaks off as a young man with a very pronounced limp comes lurching around the bend in the road and all but bumps into them.

"Oh shit! Hey you, watch it!" she cries instead and jumps back as this new arrival weighed down by the large bag he is carrying suddenly loses his balance and topples over into a heap.

The two girls look down at him in shock for a moment and then Cerys leans over him, concern evident in her voice.

"Alright, it's alright, you're okay … just get your breath back."

The man squirms as Cerys helps to extricate him from the straps of the bag. She can see that he's far from old, indeed she'd put him only a few years older than herself, but he's lean and unkempt with an unruly mop of brown hair that has fallen across a face that is surprisingly handsome. She smiles at him reassuringly and he looks back at her with deep-set eyes of the most brilliant green and then blushes. Whether from her smile or sheer mortification at finding himself in this position, Cerys suspects both and understands instinctively that less would be best in this case, she pulls the hefty bag to one side and says.

"There, that's better!"

At this most unexpected almost bizarre turn of events Delyth responds in keeping with her usual character and bursts into peals of mocking laughter.

"Oh *Duw*! But I've seen it all *now*! Nurse Cerys in action! Laura bloody Ashley the paramedic! Getting some practice in, are you, sis, or should that be *Sister Cerys?* Oh for God's sake, leave him alone, you don't know where he's *been*!"

She wrinkled her nose in disgust, "Peasant!" she spat.

"Another bloody walking sob-story thinking people will feel sorry for him! They should all stay in the cities where they have food banks and soup kitchens rather than scrounging off good honest folk like us!"

Cerys spun around in a rare burst of anger.

"DELYTH!"

Her step-sister jumps in surprise. She wasn't used to being shouted at; especially by Cerys. She stares at her in disbelief.

"Delyth, I'm telling you! Home! NOW!"

The change from gentle road-side administrator all but cooing over the fallen man has been replaced by a side that Delyth knew better than to bandy with and she thrusts out her glossy bottom lip instead.

"Alright, alright!" she replies sulkily. "Keep your hippy hair on!" Cerys flashes her a warning look and Delyth takes off towards the village at a pace faster and less dignified than she'd like. As she disappears around the first row of cottages, she consoles herself with a parting shot.

"Just don't come crying to me when you catch fleas!"

Anger is replaced by embarrassment as Cerys turns back to the man.

"I'm so sorry, she doesn't mean it. She's just annoyed with me and very young for her age. I can only apologise."

She busies herself with his bag moving it further aside making more room, "There that's better. How are you feeling now, do you think you can get up?"

The young man is obviously feeling some shame of his own but he stutters his thanks and with a combined effort they get him to his feet. He gestures to his legs.

"One shorter than the other," he says tersely by way of explanation, "have been like it all my life…"

He doesn't need to finish. Cerys gives a small nod and as she looks into those luminous green eyes again she knows instinctively that she has nothing to fear from this man.

He reminds her of a sheepdog she once found on the coast road that had escaped from a local farm. It had been hit by a car and left for dead. Despite its distress and a front leg that was obviously broken, it had allowed her to lift it to the safety of her father's car, and her dad, a worrier by nature, had fussed around her the whole time fearing she would be bitten or at the very least nipped, but the dog made no fuss such was its trust for her and Cerys never feared for one moment that she would feel those sharp teeth on her flesh. Her actions also saved the dog's life, but he never worked with sheep again living out the rest of his days in front of their fire once the farmer made it clear he didn't want him back.

She gestures to a bench not far away where it sits on the corner of the village junction.

Almost directly across on the main road old Mrs Jones is watching these events with an avid eye as she waits for the bus. But her vigil for the number 22 had hardly been dull and Cerys knows with a sinking certainty that everything will be reported back to her father. Cerys waves to her and then turns back to the young man.

"It would probably be best if you could sit down for a minute. No doubt you're still probably a bit winded ... Have you walked far?"

"Just from the town," the man replies as they make their way to the seating. Cerys takes his bag. It's heavy and well-stuffed, with, she assumes, all of his worldly possessions and she feels a deep pang of pity.

"Why, that's well over eight miles! A good hike for anyone, never mind someone with..." she breaks off, and then finishes, "with such a heavy bag!"

She smiles. The man smiles back tentatively and the eyes lose a bit of their hunted look.

"Thank you, diolch," he says, "I'm not used to people being kind to me. I just hope I haven't got you into any trouble with your friend?"

"Friend! Delyth? Well she's not actually my friend, she's my step-sister, for my sins, and no, she'll not get *me* into any trouble." Cerys's smile widens, "What? For helping someone across the road? I think *not*! Her mam would definitely approve of that, as would my da. My dad is the kindest man ever and my stepmam is lovely to be fair; it's just her daughter who's the problem!"

Cerys gives a small chuckle and glancing up catches Mrs Jones glaring over in disapproval. *Oh the old folks in this village,* she thinks in amusement, *so old-fashioned.* The bus to town trundles up and stops to collect its passenger, and leaving behind a grey puff of smoke is soon out of sight.

Cerys feels strangely relaxed, although she has no idea why she should be so comfortable with a complete stranger. But just the act of having helped him and then having had the pleasure of putting Del to flight had left her with a pleasant sense of accomplishment. And besides the young man was passing through and in all likelihood she wouldn't see him again anyway, so where was the harm in making him feel human for five minutes? She wanted to be a nurse, didn't she? And being kind to people was all par for the course, surely… And so yes, Delyth wasn't far wrong, she was practising of sorts, but there was nothing else in it beyond that, and at eighteen she was a fully-grown adult and could talk to whom she chose. She chattered on.

"Getting back to Delyth; I'm not really sure what her problem is, although I think she could be unhappy not being the only child anymore, well, that's what I think anyway, and she definitely takes it out on me. And, if I am to be completely honest, I could happily throttle her some days!"

Cerys reaches out her hands and pretends to vigorously shake an imaginary neck. The man sat beside her twitches his lips and she lets out a guilty giggle and goes on.

"I know she doesn't like living in the Valleys, and that there just isn't enough going on here for her, I get that, I really do, but..." she gazes out across to the rolling hills and momentarily presses her lips together, "It's different for me, I love it here. I've lived in this village all my life and okay, nothing much goes on here, it's small, there's no shop, and everyone knows your business. But it's what you're used to, I suppose, and I will be moving on eventually... once college is done, of course, and then it'll be uni."

She pauses and then with a flap of her hand says, "Oh hark at me going on and on and I haven't even introduced myself! I'm Cerys, by the way..."

She holds out her hand and beams at him. The young man who is practically transfixed by the bright energy of this unexpected good Samaritan, takes it hesitantly, almost shyly. He wishes his hands weren't so grubby but he had washed them before leaving town that morning. He may look like a tramp but he did do his best to stay clean as was possible.

"Llyr,' he says shortly and then looks away as though confused suddenly by the social niceties.

But Cerys is pleased enough that he's offered up his name and for no reason that she can fathom decides to probe further.

"And so where do you come from, then, Llyr, if you don't mind me asking? There's nothing 'round hereabouts except for forests and farmland. Have you come far?"

There is a long moment before he answers.

"Oh here and there. I have no interesting tale to tell, nor family of which to speak of, I'm afraid. Sorry, I don't mean to be rude, but you could say that I'm no one from nowhere and that's probably the best that someone like me can lay claim to. I'm quite boring actually…"

He shifts position on the bench and wishes himself away. To be sat like this, having a conversation with this beautiful young woman who has just literally pulled him up from the dirt is up there as one of his most bizarre encounters and he doesn't feel at ease with it; it's all a bit much and he's keen to remove himself and retrieve what he can of his dignity.

"Cerys, you've been very kind, and I don't want to put on your time any longer but I need to find a place to sleep for the night before this weather moves in," he jerks his head up to the clouds that are building more thickly, "I don't suppose you'd know of anywhere, would you?"

Slightly taken aback by the abruptness of his manner Cerys ponders for a moment.

"Why, yes, of course, I know the *perfect* place! And not far from here either! See that track there that goes into the woods?" she points to a stand of trees just outside the village, "Not a third of a mile down there is a church that's been empty for donkey's years! People use the chapel now in the village and have done since the revival! It's a bit spooky, mind, supposed to be haunted and all that, but nobody goes there so at least you'll be safe."

She adds as though an afterthought, "I can take you there, if you like? Help you with your bag and stuff?"

Her offer surprises her as much as it does him, and catching his look of discomfort she trails off in embarrassment.

"Sorry, Llyr, what am I like! You must find me *awfully* forward but I just want to make sure you're okay... That was quite a tumble you took there and I'm just, well, I guess I'm just an old mother hen..."

It was her turn now to look away; she's overcome with confusion at the sense of the rapport she feels she has with this man, who is, after all a complete stranger and yet, *there's something about him.*

As though he has read her mind, Llyr reaches out and touches her hand briefly, she turns back to him and he says softly.

"It's fine, honestly, and thank you. And I'll be alright, I promise, my legs are feeling *much* better already."

The smile he gives her transforms his face into something almost beautiful and without warning she finds herself staring into the gorgeousness of those green eyes before the moment is broken by a scowling figure who bears down at them at speed.

"Hey Cerys, *Cerys!* Is this man bothering you?"

She stiffens at the sound of that familiar shouting voice and her heart takes a deep-sea dive. Oh *no*! Of all the people to come along now, Dafydd Jenkins! He looks miffed, too, and he's coming at them like the Terminator, his cheeks ruddier than normal, pale eyes like flint. The usual two sidekicks are with him but they bring up the rear at a more leisurely pace. Dai fills her vision and blocks out the sky as he looms over them like some great hulking harbinger of doom.

"Well? Is he? Do you need me to sort him out or what?"

Although he addresses the questions to Cerys, his eyes are on Llyr who freezes likes a frightened rabbit beneath the stare of the big bad wolf.

"Dai!" cries Cerys as she springs to her feet and thrusts her hands out all in one smooth movement. "What on *earth* are you on about? No, he isn't and no, I do *not*!"

Dai doesn't even acknowledge the fact she's spoken to him and maintains the hard-line stare as his fingers twitch in barely suppressed anticipation. Cerys knows where this is going and is having none of it. Adopting a protective stance, she stands with her arms out shielding Llyr behind her.

"Dai!" she all but shouts, and this time the pale orbs slide to her face and lose something of their deadly chill. "Dai," she repeats more calmly, "for God's sake, what's got into you?"

The eyes move back to Llyr and freeze again as he says with great deliberation.

"I heard you might be having trouble. That some sad fuck had pretended to take a fall so you'd feel sorry for him. Can't be too careful with scum like that on the road these days, Cerys, and bloody hell, I've got to say but he looks alright to *me!*"

"Who told you I'd be having trouble? Oh, let me guess, Delyth!" Cerys feels a surge of anger. Oh that girl! She would deal with her later.

"Look, there's no need for this, Dai, just chill, will you? Everything's fine. This man took a tumble that's all, but he's alright now, in fact, you were just on your way, weren't you?"

Dai relaxes as he sees the other man get to his feet and limp a pace or two away hoisting the bag on to his back. And Cerys, seeing the moment of confrontation has passed, breathes a little easier and lets her arms fall to her side.

"There, see? Nothing to worry about," she turns her back on him and faces Llyr, "and you know where you're going now, so everyone's happy. No need for dramas!"

Her tone is brisk and diffuses the last of any tension as her errant and most definitely unwanted knight steps back from the bench as does Llyr as he hobbles his way towards the path into the woods giving wide berth to Dai's friends who now look on with disinterest. He doesn't dare even look at Cerys, never mind voice a final thank you, he has come across hostility like this before and he knows to just keep his head down and keep moving. He disappears off into the foliage as fast as his legs can carry him, and as soon as he's out of sight, Cerys looks to Dai and his sidekicks with thinly-veiled irritation.

"Now then, if you lot have finished charging 'round the village on your white horses, I'll be off, too."

As she went to walk away, Dai caught at her arm

"Oh don't be like that! Come on, Cerys, we were just looking out for you," he adopts a cajoling tone, "and anyway, it's been ages since I've had a chance to talk to you, why don't we sit down and have a chat for a bit…"

He flicks a hand out behind him to his friends; it is the signal for them to disappear but before they even get as far as doing an about-turn, Cerys rounds on Dai.

"Two things you need to know, Dai Jenkins! First-off, there's a storm coming and I don't intend to stick around and get soaked not for you, not for anyone! And secondly, I'm not interested in having a chat with you! How many times have I got to tell you this? I'm *not* interested, Dai, I'm not interested! Now please leave me alone!"

She shakes his hand off her arm and veers around him, and as she passes the two friends they smirk at her openly but she ignores them completely and is soon gone.

Dai glares at his two companions and they straighten their mouths immediately.

"Well! What's so funny? Are you telling me neither of you two have never been knocked back before!"

He snorts and runs a meaty hand through the pale blonde crop that is bristling as much as he is, "What *is* her problem!"

"Dai, mate," says the friend called Neil, "she's just playing hard to get!"

"Nah, you're miles off," interjects the other, Tomos, otherwise known as Twm. Almost as fair as Dai but physically much smaller and the brains of the trio. None of them work except for the odd cash-in-hand with the harvests, but he is the only one who left school with any qualifications. He nods his head sagely with the air of a man who knows these things.

"It is as the lady says. She's just not interested. I mean, come on, Dai, how many years have you been trying to get into her knickers! Two? Three? Why waste your time!"

He gives a sly wink and digs at Neil with his elbow, "You might have more luck with the younger sister, though eh, Neil… eh, eh?"

It's now Neil's turn to snort and he pokes back at Twm. He's the better-looking of the trio; slim, dark, swarthy and with curls that the girls usually liked to play with. He sees himself as the village heart-throb that none can resist, with the exception of Cerys and her stepsister seemingly.

"Bloody hell, you *are* joking! All I got was a *kiss!* And just *that* after nearly a bottle of cider that *I* paid for! Thinks something of herself that one, I can tell you, but you can certainly have a go, Dai, if you don't mind a gobful of that gunk she puts on her lips!"

As he and Twm cackle in glee Dai gestures impatiently and glowers off in the direction of the village.

"I just don't understand her!" he says petulantly, "It's not as though she doesn't know me or anything, we've known each other for *years*! And I'm a safe bet; I'd make sure I looked after her."

"Yeah, you'd look after her alright!" Neil chimes in. "And maybe it's the fact that she *does* know you, Dai, that's the problem!"

As he and Twm dissolve into fits of laughter Dai flushes an ugly red as he realises the depths of this rejection. She's made him look a right bloody fool! *Can sit and chat with some low-life off the street all morning and play the nice nurse when it suits her, but she can't be bothered to spend a minute talking to me!* And what did that piece of scum have that he doesn't, anyway?

Inwardly Dai starts ticking off his fingers as though by doing so he can compensate for the humiliation in some way. He's fit. He works out. He plays rugby and doesn't go mad for the booze – just the usual sesh on the weekend. And he does intend to get a job, there's just nothing out there for him at the moment, and besides, he does alright with bits here and there. He just doesn't get it. And he likes her, as in he *really likes her a lot*! He just wishes she'd give him a chance to prove how good he could be to her and *for* her.

As a rule, she evaded his clumsy attempts with good-natured tact, always careful not to hurt his feelings. But today she let fly in a way he had never seen before. And besides, she'd totally shown him up in front of his friends, the directness of her response had wounded him deeply, and no girl, no matter how lovely, should have the power of *that*!

His pride has well and truly been kicked into touch, but he still wants her. God, how he wants her...

With an effort he breaks free of these thoughts but his mood is low and has become as dark and as ominous as the louring sky. There is a murmur of thunder and he glances over towards the woods. He knows exactly where the cripple has gone. But the rain has now started and his business will keep.

He turns towards the village. His companions are still standing about sniggering at some private joke, but Dai has had enough entertainment for one day at his expense and favours them both with a dead-arm as he passes. At the sound of their howls he feels his mood lift significantly and breaking into a steady jog, calls over his shoulder, "Not so funny now, is it? Come on, you two; stop screaming like a pair of girls!"

He gives a hoot of laughter, "And I'll have the bloody last laugh as well, you'll see!"

His friends eye each other ruefully as they rub their arms and then as the storm sweeps in they run before it and career along the village street as though the Devil himself were after them. Dai sees them run past his house and enter Twm's further up. They're obviously not happy with him but they'll get over it, he thinks, and besides, it'll teach them not to take the piss. His mam is talking to him, commenting on the change in the weather and if he wants anything.

She's been baking. Savoury aromas fill the cottage and he manages an amiable smile. Good as gold, his mam! Shame Cerys wasn't more like her. And stuff Neil and Twm! He has other friends. Once this storm has blown over he plans to get the bus into town and get bladdered.

And so, yes please, mam, can he have an early tea? Best I line my stomach if I want a clear head in the morning, eh? And his mother seeing the glint in those eyes so like his two older brothers, has no inclination to enquire further as to this statement and nor does she want to know. Her philosophy is that some things are better left unsaid, and others well alone. Her son, however, shared neither of these sentiments and his thoughts are busy as he stares out of the window.

# Chapter 3

The young man called Llyr stumbles into the clearing and comes to a halt at the sight of the church. It's small, crumbly and looks more ancient than he expected. Weeds and creeping ivy have taken possession of its grey walls, and the trees above cast deep darkening shadows. He stops and allows his bag to drop as looked back towards the path but no one had followed him and he moves hesitantly towards the weather-beaten doors that still looked surprisingly sturdy.

One is slightly ajar, as though inviting him in, and he doesn't know why but he's suddenly overcome by a feeling of acute apprehension. He stops again looks about him as though hoping for alternative shelter; but there is only the old church and he doesn't fancy traipsing back to the village.

The sun goes in as clouds swiftly gather, and a rumble of thunder mutters in the distance as the golden light of the day all but seeps away, as though drained by the arrival of something more sinister than a summer storm. As the shadows deepen around the old stone building, the young man takes a deep breath and seems to arrive at a decision, and gripping his bag firmly he limps his way across the clearing to the doors. He pushes at the one that stands ajar and it creaks loudly but gives easily enough and he takes his first look inside.

There isn't much to see amidst the gloom; just some old broken benches discoloured by damp and years of mildew, a stone-slabbed floor carpeted with old leaves and the spoor of small animals. He looks up to the one large stained glass window that sits above the broken stone altar and sees the gesturing figure of a man surrounded by administering angels, but the colours are faded and a large crack zigzags its way through the middle. Drawn to the tableau he looks more closely at the man depicted there who gazes back mournfully and he can understand why nobody from the village comes here and believes the place to be haunted. The shadows are deep but seem *aware,* and within them sits a singular silence as though the old church has been expecting him and is holding its breath. Llyr is reluctant to enter any further. It may've been hallowed ground once but there's eeriness about it and he continues to linger in the doorway. He is afraid but he doesn't know why. Something doesn't feel right and he's learned to trust his instincts. His body cries out for rest and he knows his options are limited.

The storm is all but upon him, flashing fire and bellowing rage like some vengeful dragon roaring across the skies, but it is the first splatters of rain that decide him and he propels himself forward leaving the door slightly ajar.

He makes his way slowly and painfully up towards what had been the stone altar and it sits like two great broken fangs atop the altar steps and he wonders fleetingly, how it came to be in that state. He jumps as the storm dragon sears through the church with a white shocking light and for a moment every dark corner is revealed. But it is enough for Llyr to see that nothing else lurks within the shadows and, feeling greatly reassured, some of the tension begins to leave his body.

Another grumble of thunder precedes another flash and he relaxes further but not without a slight twinge of shame although it's not the storm that's bothering him. It's just an old church for Christ's sake! Dropping his bag with a hefty thump, he says loudly to himself, "You've slept in worse than *this,* Llyr! Come on, get a grip, mun!"

It was the only way; to face the fear and get on with it. Hadn't that always been the story of his life! And besides, where else was there for him to go? He could go back into the village, he supposed, but the thought of getting caught out in the storm – not to mention the local bully-boys, was distinctly unappealing and at least here he would be dry and remain in one piece! He makes an uneasy peace with his decision; he would stay. The church for all that it felt odd was still, to all intents and purposes, a house of God, so what is there to be scared of? But the fear remains, nevertheless, it has just been pushed down like the well-trained dog it is and brought to heel.

Llyr knew as much as anyone who lived a precarious street existence, that fear became your constant companion whether you liked it or not. It went with you everywhere like an unwelcome but essential shadow. It ate with you, walked with you, slept with you, it remained at your side no matter what. On the plus side it could also warn of unseen and hidden dangers and provide unexpected protection; Llyr knew the beast well, and the fact it would also consume you if you allowed it free rein.

In a bid to provide some semblance of further reassurance he recalls the sleepless night he spent at an old psychiatric hospital up in Denbighshire a few of Winters ago. Now *that* place was spooky, and if it wasn't for the fact that there were others who had breached security and found a niche like himself that night, he swears he wouldn't have stayed there, snow or no snow! Somewhat comforted by what he deemed a favourable comparison, Llyr got down to business and scanned the church for a suitable spot to sleep. He decides to make camp at the foot of the three altar steps, that way, he reckons, he can still see the doors and keep an eye on that altar maw in case it gets hungry in the night...

Inwardly he chastises his imagination but the act of organising his bed settles him down as the rain descends in a deluge and drums loudly on the old slate roof. Llyr whistles softly and the sound echoes eerily.

"Got out of that in time! Bloody hell, I would've got soaked!" he mutters and let loose a soft chuckle. It's nerves, he knows, but just hearing a voice, even if it is his own addressing something as banal as the weather lends an air of normality and he chuckles some more, "Talking to yourself now, Llyr, people will think you're bloody *twp!*"

His sleeping bag now unfurled, he groans as he lowers himself down on to it and then sits rubbing his legs as he looks about him.

"Well if there are any ghosties about I'll just be here for the night, alright? I just need some kip, and then I'll be gone by the morning, okay?"

The thunder rumbles back at him but only half-heartedly as the storm begins to move away.

*Wow, that was short but sweet!* Thinks Llyr, and then his thoughts turned to Cerys and how she stuck up for him. Why she'd even want to bother he had no idea, but he was grateful that her actions had spared him a possible beating. It was comforting to know that there were still some *good* people out there in the world who were willing to champion a lost cause. And he was a lost cause, there was no mistake about that!

Orphaned at an early age and sent to an institution where he was supposed to be cared for, looked after and nurtured, but where things happened ... *bad* things ... Abruptly he shifts position as though by doing so he can shake off the memories that plague him like thieves in the night. Llyr banishes them back to a dark room within himself and almost guiltily begins to think of Cerys again with her loose flowing hair and her kind, clear eyes that somehow seemed to *understand* him. He tried to analyse that brief but tangible connection between them, for it was as though she sensed all the tribulations within him and that it didn't matter, but that somehow, incredibly, amazingly, *he did!*

It had been a defining moment for him, practically momentous – for no one had looked at him like that since before his parents has died, and after so many years of living in a lonely and emotional wilderness it was a rare thing to encounter interest that was genuine.

And in a moment of unprecedented self-indulgence he draws pleasure from the memory and in the next dismisses it with his customary self-deprecation. She wasn't interested in *him,* for Christ's sake! What would she be interested in him for! He was a coward and a cripple with nothing to offer other than a painful past and a life spent wandering. He had intrigued her for a few moments and that was all. Or at least his eyes had. They were his best feature, after all, or so he'd been told. But he's smart enough to know that girls always wanted more than just a nice pair of eyes which was why he usually avoided them and besides, he was hardly a catch, was he!

Life was less complicated on his own and more fool he if even thought for *just* one second that a girl as beautiful as Cerys could feel more than pity in her heart for the likes of him! Kindness came easily to people like her; it was the ones who offered kindness with an agenda you need to watch. He smiles sardonically as he rearranges his pillow, that is his coat. He's known a few 'kind' Samaritans in his time. All concern and good intentions until you feel their hands in your pockets, or in places they shouldn't be...

He shudders and with a concerted effort drives the thoughts away. *Enough brooding, time to sleep! All in all, it's not been a bad day, so why spoil it?*

As his weary body finally gives in to the exertions of the day, he clasps his hands behind his head and unwittingly he sees Cerys in his mind once again, her freshness, her prettiness, the strength of her character as she faced Goliath; a gorgeous girl, in a class of her own and such guts...

With a sigh he releases the image and with it all tensions of the day and the gloom in the church dissipates a little as the sun comes back out and soon Llyr is yawning on the cusp of sleep. He shifts position and pulls his blanket up over him. It isn't particularly cold, if anything the interior of the church is surprisingly warm for such an old and damp place, but he doesn't dwell on this, indeed the strangeness of this fact has barely registered.

The thunder mumbles again faintly in the distance and a strand of watery sunlight finds its way through the trees outside and through the stained glass.

This single ray enhances the features of the gesturing man and his face becomes almost animated. And just before Llyr gives in to complete exhaustion, it suddenly comes to him that the figure *was* Jesus, and that the eyes, which had previously looked out into the church and beyond had moved just ever so slightly and were looking straight down at him; and there was a great sorrow in them.

Sometime later, as Llyr breathed evenly and descended into the deeper echelons of blissful sleep, the day began to wend its way gradually into evening as the birds sing their last hymns for the night. Something stirs in the darkening gloom and from the shadows come the souls who had been lost, but are lost no more. They glide slowly over to the sleeping figure and regard him in silence. After some moments they look to each other and then move off towards the cracked altar before disappearing into the gaping hole and the depths below.

Llyr sleeps on oblivious to their visit and dreams of stained glass windows where the figures move and come to life. He sleeps for several hours until he wakes suddenly. For several seconds he thinks he's still dreaming as the light has faded and the muted colours of Jesus and his angels have receded into dark shapes, and he casts about for his bag before rummaging for his torch. He finds it but it clicks uselessly and he remembers he'd needed new batteries almost a week ago and inwardly cursed himself. A further forage in the bag then saw him produce a box of matches and he strikes a flame quickly before applying it to a thick, stumpy candle he always carries for such emergencies. The flame gutters and weaves before settling into a feeble glow, but it is enough to show him the figure that sits just inches away.

Gasping with fright he lurches back awkwardly trying to put as much distance as possible between himself and this mystery watcher.

"Wha... wha... hey!" he slips and he scrambles madly but the blanket has trapped him and so he leans back, half upright, the candle held wavering before him.

"Calm yourself. There's nothing to be afraid of..." comes a soothing voice out of the darkness.

It's female. The tone is light, the inflection honed to reassure and Llyr is immediately on his guard. A woman? In this place? Alone in the middle of the night! He wonders if he's still dreaming and peers to get a closer look, as all the while his periphery vision is scanning for others.

The light doesn't give him much but he sees more than shadow and the woman who hunches before him on the steps is striking. She has a mane of light hair that cascades around her making her look almost faerie-like, and for some reason Llyr's feelings of unease increase manifold. She watches him as he watches her, but whereas he's filled with concern and curiosity, the woman in comparison is relaxed and seems completely unperturbed. She also appears to be waiting for him to speak, and clearing his throat nervously Llyr fumbles to explain himself.

"I'm sorry... I didn't realise there was anyone else here, I was... er... well... I would've moved on had I known, so I'll ... er... just get my stuff together and I'll be gone."

The woman holds up a hand, "Don't go on my account, it really is no bother. You're welcome to stay as long as you like."

She flashes him a smile that all but takes his breath away, and he notices she has the most beautifully coloured eyes like warm honey. *But who is she? And where has she come from?* As these questions rise to his lips she pre-empts him by extending a pale hand and despite being full of misgivings, he leans out and gives it a small shake.

"Sarah. Welcome to my church." she says pleasantly. Her hands feel cool, the fingers long and tapering.

"I'm Llyr... and I'm sorry to be trespassing," he knows it to be a lame and bizarre response but his mind is still trying to work things out. She unnerves him in a way that suggests it may be better (safer?) to play along and if she says it's her church who is he to argue! Keep things sweet, he thinks, and then make his exit as soon as possible.

"Llyrrr…" she rolls the 'r' with all the sensuality of a lazy cat and then lets out a low, musical laugh, "Why I haven't heard that name in years!"

Her correct pronunciation of his name surprises him as he detected no Welshness at all in her voice and he wonders where she's from.

"A good Welsh name. A fine one, indeed, and named after the God of the Sea," She fixes him with the honeyed eyes and he's not sure whether they're innocent or mocking him, "Are you from the sea, then, Llyrrr...?"

He drags his gaze away aware that his discomfort is now giving way to feelings of real anxiety. Who is she? What's going on? And more to the point, what kind of a question is that! He briefly sweeps the church with worried eyes almost expecting to see someone creeping up on him but there are only deep shadows and a strange stillness in the air, "Er… No, but look, I really should be going, as you say, it's your church, so…"

"So then where are you from, young man?" she cuts in, the smile is still there but he hears the slight edge in the voice and knows to tread carefully. He tries to relax. Just humour her for a bit; he tells himself, she's obviously got a screw or two loose and probably wanders around like this just to freak out the locals. And he could believe it, too, with her white witchy hair and the odd black dress – or was it because he *wanted* to believe it! *You've met all kinds and worse than this.*

*Come on, boyo,* he admonished himself, *box clever and we'll soon be out of here.*

"A place called Abermaigrl, just up the coast. Nowhere special, just your typical one-horse village..." He attempts a laugh but it comes out more of a croak, "And you ... you're from the village?"

She nods imperceptibly, a faint quirk around the lips, and then putting her head almost coyly to one side she says, "Ahhh... so you are from *near* the sea, but not *from* the sea... and so if you are not the Welsh God of the Sea as you have been named for, Llyrrrrrr..." she rolls the 'r's even further this time and a number of thoughts flash through his mind, the main one being that this weird white-haired lady of the church was more than just crazy, and that the next time he had a bad feeling about a place he would *listen* and then just keep walking, storm or not!

"Then perhaps you are a God anyway..." she went on in a tone that had become almost wondering, as though by voicing her thoughts she was drawing some kind of conclusion?

"...Only you just never realised it before and yet now here you are... and so are you? Are you a god, Llyr...?"

He looks at her blankly. There are no words he can find to formulate an answer but he senses some kind of a response is expected and that it would go ill against him if he fails to find one, "A god! Me? Oh, I *wish!*"

He tries another laugh and this time, much to his surprise, it sounds more natural and his sense of relief is huge as the woman joins in. He puts the candle down and seizes the moment, extricating himself from the blanket he rolls it up. He has little outside of his bag to pack, and he means to stuff things in quickly and make good his exit. This conversation has gone far enough!

Sarah reaches out and grabs his arm, "Wait!"

It is a command not a request, and an orange glint flares in her eyes lending them a strange fierceness. Gone are the sweet, sugary depths that had at first enthralled him, now in their place are a sly, predatory and menacing light.

"Wait..." She says more softly, and pinning him with a force of will he'd never experienced before, she leans in and lowers her voice. The fires in her eyes are banked down and now glow with an irresistible allure. Llyr is drawn in despite himself and now feels a thrill of a different kind. The woman who introduced herself as Sarah releases his arm and moved her hand up to his face, tracing his features with one finger, her touch light and spidery thin.

"How many times has this beautiful face looked out upon the world in the hope of a better tomorrow, only for the world to turn theirs away, because of *this*!"

Fast as lightening her hand whips down to his afflicted leg and he jumps but doesn't dare pull away.

"And how many times, in the sleepless hours of night, have you buried your dreams like cherished treasure and yet prayed for a miracle that would make you a better man, a *different* man! To be able to stride amongst others like the giant you truly are; tall, strong and *straight!*"

Llyr's face flickers and she nods, "All of your life you have had to endure the taunts and the gibes, the stares and the pity. To falter when you would walk, to fall when you would run... What kind of a life is that for a young man as virile and as handsome as *you!*"

He blushes, both emotionally captivated and embarrassed and would've dropped his eyes if he could but she has him well in her sights and he cannot break away.

"Ahhh how you blush... but look how fine you are... the face! The eyes! The mouth that has never been kissed! You fear to love and bare your heart and by doing so have denied yourself all of Life's *greatest* pleasures!"

She smiles and her hand begins to stroke his leg gently as her voice takes on a hypnotic quality, "Let us fix you, let us heal you, let us make this *right*... why bury yourself with all your dreams when the miracle you've always wanted lies just within your reach...?" With a surge of frightened courage Llyr had managed to shift back and loosen her hold on his leg, but his attempts to speak were less successful. His tongue feels alien and turgid like it doesn't belong to him anymore, and his thoughts are disjointed like an incomplete jigsaw puzzle. He struggles to rise, all of his instincts on the deepest levels are in full cry but it's as though he's pinned in the paws of some great beast as the very life-force is drained out of him.

"Don't fight it," the woman takes his face in her hands, "Don't fight it, Llyr..."

His vision becomes blurry as an innate heaviness steals over him, as his limbs turn to lead, but his eyes remain open and captivated by those of the woman for now they seem to have grown huge and (*orange?*) like great glowing lamps. How could he ever have thought they were beautiful when they were all but consuming him with their ominous intent. They're *hungry* eyes; evil eyes, and the image of the great yawning maw of the altar flashes before him as fear gives way to a sense of doom. He feels as though he is falling but the hands that had cupped his face have moved and are firmly assisting him back down to his bed.

Fatigue creeps over him like he'd never known before, there is no resistance as he succumbs gradually and the world around him turns grey. The woman who was once known as Sarah smiles down at him and scolds him gently,

"There, there, Llyr, hush now. No need to fuss... you are amongst friends now."

She reaches across and unfurls the blanket before draping it over his comatose form, "Sleep now and dream of greatness, my beauty," her smile widens as she touches his cheek with a tender, possessive caress, and as he stirs briefly she coos lovingly, "Oh yes, dare to dream, handsome, and of a life more fitting, a life more fulfilling... a life more *fair*! And we'll give that to you and more... *much* more, Llyr! Oh yes..."

She leans down and puts her lips to his ear, "For we can make *all* dreams come true... so come to us... stay with us... and I promise you, we'll make you a God amongst men..."

# Chapter 4

Cerys was up bright and early the next morning and, as the rest of the house slept on, she has a quick breakfast of tea and cereal and then makes up a flask of coffee. Her intention is to visit Llyr at the old church before he departs on the next stage of his journey and a hot drink would be most welcome to send him on his way. Some fruit, biscuits and a hastily made sandwich also disappear into the bag holding the flask, and putting on her all-weather red hooded mac she slips out of the house and into a damp drizzly morning.

She shivers and pulls her hood up as she hurries along and knows she wouldn't hear the last of it if Delyth got wind of what she was doing.

The village is deserted except for Mr Thomas's tabby cat making its way home through the neighbours' gardens. Glancing briefly up at the leaden skies Cerys thinks what a shame the lovely weather has had to come to an end, but term time would be starting in a couple of weeks' time and wasn't that always the way! She passes Dai Jenkins' house and as usual kept her eyes forward. The fact he is seriously sweet on her and has been for some years was common knowledge, and after his macho display yesterday Cerys was keener than ever to keep him at arm's length.

Unknown to her however, she, too, was in his thoughts, as unseen and tucked behind the curtains upstairs Dai has an excellent view as the subject of favourite imaginings scuttles past, for he, along with every villager on the street would know that bright red coat anywhere and the person within it. Cerys!

Dai Jenkins Junior had been as good as his word; had duly got bladdered and woke early with a hangover he could handle with his erstwhile objective still fresh in his mind and a mulish determination to see it through. He just happened to be coming back from dispensing the results of last night's beer when a flash of red caught his eye across the road. And there, can you believe it was Cerys! But where was she going and what was she carrying in the bag? A dull anger made his head throb suddenly and his fists clenched as even he, with his limited intelligence and lack of academia, could figure it out.

She was bound for the church, and that piece of vermin lurking within. No doubt there were goodies in the bag for the poor crippled sod – God; she was such a soft touch! He reined himself in with an effort. No point poking his nose in, though – not at this stage. She'd just get mad and tear a strip off him and he wasn't sure his pride could take that again so soon. And besides, he hadn't given up in his quest for her, for in his mind she was more than spoken for – she was already his. But if he was to win her over, then he'd have to be clever and tread carefully. Traits that didn't come naturally and he knew it.

Cerys meanwhile went along the path into the woods like a modern-day Little Red Riding Hood bearing, as had her fairy tale counterpart, a simple gift of food and good intent. The smells around her were organically rich from the recent rainfall and she breathes in deeply, happy to be out of the house and on, what she deems a secret mercy mission. Soon the church is in sight, and she checks herself, as does everyone else when the old grey walls came into view. She isn't so much afraid of the folklore as respectful of local opinion. It is a sad and sorry sight but then it hadn't been used in nearly a hundred years or so.

She slows to a stop as she comes into the clearing and sees the doors shut before her. She wonders if he may be asleep. She glances at her heart-shaped watch and sees it's just after eight. Did homeless people sleep in on Sundays? Or was it just like another day? The thought arrests her for a moment, but there was only one way to find out. Stepping up to the weathered wood she knocks tentatively feeling rather foolish, but good manners indicate the action whether Llyr is in residence or not. And after several seconds of hearing nothing at all she raps more loudly and hears a faint, "Come in…?"

Cerys tests the doors and finds one to be more giving. She pushes and it groans and stepping into the gloom she espies Llyr immediately, huddled on the altar steps with a blanket wrapped around him, his bag at his feet. His face when he sees her is a myriad of different emotions; surprise, pleasure, and not a little confusion.

"Good morning, bore da!" Cerys holds up the thick carrier bag, "I've brought you some breakfast!" Llyr now looks openly bewildered as Cerys comes towards him with an assured step. She flicks her gaze briefly around the church and seems unimpressed; but in a *good* way and for some unknown reason this heartens him, yet he still can't find his tongue.

"You survived the ghosts, then?" says Cerys jauntily, "or did they scare you speechless in the night!"

She winks and he realises she's joking.

He shakes his head wonderingly and runs a hand through his thick hair, "Forgive me, you startled me. I didn't expect... I never thought..." He peels off and offers a sheepish smile, "Bore da, and thank you, as if you haven't been kind enough."

Cerys waves a hand dismissively and places the bag at his feet, "Oh it's no problem. There's some coffee in there – thought it might've been a bit chilly in the night and there's also some..." she broke off suddenly, "what the...?"

Her mouth drops open as she spots the broken altar and turns to Llyr with a look of shock. He lifts his thin shoulders.

"I have no idea. It was like that when I arrived. Seems strange but maybe there was a weakness in the rock that just gave way or something," he shrugs again, "Who knows..."

And for some inexplicable reason he wants to warn her as she trips lightly up the steps for a closer look. He watches her anxiously as she approaches the stone... *Maw?*

"Oh my God," breathes Cerys, "it's cracked right through…" and stretching forward she leans in to get a better look. Llyr watches her uneasily and feels an overwhelming urge to warn her although he doesn't know why. It's this place; he thinks worryingly, there's something weird about it.

He'd woken up early feeling slightly off-colour. Not ill, as such but he'd felt tired, listless and bit foggy round the brain. As far as he was aware he'd slept alright but there had been dreams, strange dreams. Dreams of… Seeing Cerys leaning in even further, Llyr can't contain himself any longer.

"Hey Cerys, I hope you're going to have a cup of this coffee with me? I have my own mug so you can use the one on the flask if you like!"

His voice sounds unnaturally cheery and loud and it echoes slightly but it has the desired effect. Distracted by this pleasant but unexpected offer, Cerys turns immediately towards him as he pulls the flask out of the bag and proffers it towards her.

"Well, if you're sure… I mean, I had brought it for you." Llyr waggles the flask and she gives a small laugh, "Oh go on, then!"

Giving the altar a final glance she joins Llyr on the steps with a respectable distance between them. As he delves into his bag for his travel mug she unscrews the flask and after pouring for them both holds her plastic cup aloft, *"Iechyd da!"*

Despite himself and the strange mood he's in, Llyr breaks open into another smile and tips his mug, *"Iechyd da."*

God but he likes her! So kind, so funny! The incongruence of sitting in an old church having coffee with such a lovely girl strikes him as funny and he gives a rare chuckle that is a mixture of disbelief and delight.

"What?"

He has surprised her twice in as many minutes, and further intrigued by this odd young man, Cerys smiles to see mirth in those beautiful green eyes and gets it immediately. She laughs with him and they share a moment; it's only a small one but it dissipates the tension and both visibly begin to relax.

Taking a sip of coffee Cerys gestures around the church, "So how was it, then? Did you manage to get some kip after?"

"I did – surprisingly," says Llyr, "although the dreams were odd…"

Twisting around he looks up at the figures in the stained glass window and, intrigued, Cerys follows his gaze.

"I know this is going to sound crazy but… but it was like they all came to life in the glass last night and tried to talk to me." Llyr nods at Jesus, "Him especially… all a bit weird, really, and I still haven't a clue what they were trying to say!"

He laughs nervously and turns back to his coffee.

Cerys follows suit, "Well, it's bound to be a bit bizarre spending the night in a church – especially one as old as this one. I mean, look at it! Just the bare bones really and nothing left except…" she turns and glances back with a frown, "the old altar. But I don't understand it. It wasn't like this the last time I came in here. It's like a kind of sacrilege, isn't it, when something like that gets defaced... Do you think it was deliberate?"

"I have no idea," Llyr replies honestly, "Maybe some kids high on drugs came in and had a mad moment with a sledgehammer or something, I don't know... so what's the story with this place anyway?"

He's still keen to remove her attention from that waiting maw and to his relief Cerys takes the bait.

"The story? Oh the ghost story, you mean. Here..."

She leans across and pulls the sandwiches from out the bag, "Ham – my dad's favourite and not cheap so dig in! There's also some biscuits and other stuff to keep you going." Llyr accepts the foil-covered package gratefully and opens it.

"You were saying... about this place and the ghost story?"

"The *ghosts*, you mean!" corrects Cerys and is pleased to see him tuck into the bread and ham. *God, he must be starving, poor bugger! He also looked so pale this morning,* she observes, *perhaps he didn't sleep as well as he claimed* and she feels a twinge of guilt. It was she who told him the old church was haunted. *Not one of your better moments, Cerys,* she tells herself, *sometimes the less said the better!* She began.

"Well, back in the 1600's when all the witch-hunts were going on, there was a farm several miles from here where the daughter of the house allegedly had strange powers. Nothing was much thought of it, local country folk were generally more relaxed about it apparently. So anyway, she and the family were pretty much left to get on with their lives until one day the daughter crossed paths with some young man at the village fair and was smitten. He, too, was quite taken but he was already betrothed to another."

She pauses to take a sip of coffee and goes on.

"Well, the story has it that the daughter was beside herself with longing for this man, pursued him until he agreed to meet with her. She was determined to have him and worked 'her wiles' apparently to win him over. And he, the poor man – or should that be *stupid* man?" Cerys grins at Llyr mischievously, "didn't stand a chance. And so when he broke off his engagement it caused quite a scandal, not least because the young woman he was supposed to marry also happened to be the minister's daughter!" Llyr pauses in the act of chewing and raises his eyebrows. Cerys nods meaningfully.

"Yes, you can imagine! But the minister's daughter was no pushover and went after her rival in more ways than one and found out where she lived. With her father and some members of *his* family, they paid a visit and there was a big scene where she ended up accusing the farmer's daughter of witchcraft, no less!" Cerys shakes her head disbelievingly.

"Now that's what I'd call a woman scorned! Because for seducing her man and luring him away from her, she threw at her the only thing she could. And because of the hysteria going on at that time, even as far into Wales as this – it was dangerous, if not a death sentence to be branded as such, but the minister's daughter obviously decided that if she wasn't going to have him – then no one else would!"

She gave a wry smile, "Very Christian, eh, but without a doubt the ultimate revenge and there was no messing about either because on that very same day they sent word to the authorities apparently."

She takes up the flask and tops up his coffee, "So, the farmer's daughter, for all that she was guilty of stealing another woman's man, and this was probably her *only* crime, had *no* chance! And she was up against it, alright. A minister of the church, the well-connected family, they were even able to bring the errant beau back into line. But sadly it was too late for Sarah…"

"Who?" Llyr sat up straight and Cerys looks at him in bemusement.

"Sarah. The farmer's daughter."

"The witch, you mean…" says Llyr and immediately doesn't know why he said it. His face has a puzzled look now matched by the one Cerys is wearing and she waits for him to finish, "Sorry, I don't know why I said that… but she was a witch… wasn't she?"

Cerys pulled a face.

"Bloody hell, Llyr, nicking someone else's boyfriends doesn't make every woman who does it a witch, you know!"

"Yeah, yeah, I know, sorry. Guess I was just really into the story."

But he knows it's something more but he just can't put his finger on it. A woman… *the woman…* a witch? *What woman for heaven's sake! And why did he react to the name? He doesn't even know a Sarah! What the hell's wrong with you, Llyr!* he admonishes himself. He cast a troubled look about the church; *it'll be a long time before he'll ever spend a night in a place like this again,* he thinks, *perhaps never. Talk about messing with your head!* He shakes the thoughts off and listens as Cerys takes back up with the story.

"But of course we'll never know if she really was a witch because it never went to trial. In fact, *she* never went to trial... she made sure of that!"

Llyr made a questioning gesture, "Why was that – did she do a runner? Take off with this guy and live happily ever after or something...?"

"No, if only it had been that easy. As soon as she got word the Witch-Finders were on their way she left the farm and went for a walk... a long one; she never came back," Llyr isn't aware he's stopped breathing as Cerys pauses and lowers her voice.

"She ensured she'd inflict the ultimate revenge and hung herself from a tree right outside this church... It was her final statement, a last powerful act of defiance, because it was *the minister's* church! And as if committing such a forbidden act on holy ground wasn't bad enough, the fact she took her life on *his* doorstep! An accusation in itself and directed at both him *and* his daughter. Very clever, devious almost, and what a state she must've been in to have done a thing! All very sad and dramatic. So there you have it..." Cerys straightens up and finishes her coffee as Llyr let out his breath in a long, low whistle,

*"Iesu Grist*, that was some story! And so is it her then, who's supposed to haunt the church? This... Sarah?"

Again the name reverberates within some corner of his mind but he still feels sluggish, despite the coffee.

"You're kidding, aren't you!" Cerys shifts position and pulls her coat more tightly about her, "Taking your own life in those days was considered the worst thing possible, in fact I think it still is, because believe me, back in the day neither your body *nor* your spirit would be allowed to even *touch* hallowed ground! Local legend has it she was buried in the woods – in unconsecrated ground, of course, so, no, I don't think it would be *her* ghost in the church. Definitely not!"

"Then who, or what does…?" Llyr persists and Cerys looks at him askance. He seems to be taking an unusual interest and there is now a slightly agitated air about him.

"Llyr, it's just an old wives' tale. You know what it's like, people get hold of an old scandal, they dress it up, make it scarier and bingo! You've got your ghost story! It's the same all over. The only reason the villagers stopped using this church was because the chapel in the village when it was built was nearer, and, well… oh alright!"

She sighs.

"If you really want to know; the story goes that it is the minister and his daughter who haunt this place, along with the family of her lover because in order to save face, they'd also joined in with the accusations apparently. It's said that none of them can rest because it was their false testimony that drove her to her death. Guess the saying, guilty until proven innocent was pretty much how things were dealt with in those days, eh…?"

She smiles at him, "But it is *just* a story, Llyr, a tragic one, I'll grant you but it's just an old myth." Llyr looks thoughtful and then asks, "So do you believe it, then, Cerys... this myth?"

"It's a very old story. Who knows whether it was true or not, I grew up with it, as did all the children in these parts, and to be honest, I just think it's been used as a means to keep us away from the place. It's old and crumbly and not the safest playground you'd want your kids to be fooling around in, and so no, I don't buy it, not really."

She glances at her watch, "Whoops, is that the time! I'd love to stay more and chat, but I'd best be getting back." She stands up and stretching turns to look up at the stained glass window, and in a bid to lighten the atmosphere, says, "Well at least you had *him* looking out for you! No wonder you weren't disturbed by any spooks in the night – not if he'd got your back!"

She picks up the flask and gives it a shake.

"There's still coffee in here so I'll leave you finish it, Llyr. Perhaps you could leave the flask just inside the doors when you go and I'll collect it another time?" Llyr nods and then looks up as Cerys extends a hand out to him. He takes it gently.

"Well it's been an odd encounter, but a very nice one, and I really do wish you all the best. Take care of yourself, Llyr, won't you?"

He looks up at her and they regard each other for a few moments before he squeezes her hand just slightly and then lets it go. He feels terribly deflated as though he's lost a part of himself.

"Thank you for everything, Cerys, even the ghost story. I've really enjoyed your company. And your kindness has meant *so* much... *diolch.*"

"*Croeso*, you're more than welcome. And hey... you never know, maybe good luck is waiting 'round the corner and things will get better."

She lit his heart a final time with a warm smile saying, "In fact, let that be my farewell wish to you and that things *will get better*! *Hwyl fawr*, Llyr..."

He watches as she walks briskly towards the doors with a rising sense of deep regret that threatens to choke him. She looks back briefly and then slips through the doors and is gone.

He looks down at her empty cup on the step and then to his own and decides that he doesn't want any more coffee. It just doesn't feel the same now that Cerys has gone. She was like a bright light and as soon as she left he feels as though the church has grown darker, his spirits more depleted, and his head stuffed and to the brim with unanswered questions, foolish dreams and an unfathomable despair. He needs to get out of here; it's time to go.

He pulls the blanket from around his shoulders and raises himself awkwardly from the cold stone steps. Using his water bottle he sluices out his mug and then shoves it along with the stuff Cerys has brought him into his bag. As usual the pain in his hips flares up as he starts to slowly but doggedly limp his way out. But he's used to the pain, it's like an old companion and he focuses on it almost gladly rather than the ache that's in his heart, and as he comes out of the church and into the clearing he has nothing more on his mind than the need to find a bush and relieve himself, and then he looks up and sees Dai Jenkins.

## Chapter 5

Soft drizzle and a general feeling of wetness all over were the first sensations Llyr feels when he finally comes to. And then came the pain. Great waves of it and he groans as he realises he can only open one eye, and even then, barely. His face is a mass of pain and his ribs feel as though they'd been jumped on from a great height. As he went to lick his lips his tongue tastes blood and a few teeth move in their sockets and his jaw, oh dear Lord, his jaw. Bloody hell, he had taken a beating, but why it had been so savage he could only guess. And as the face of his assailant rise up before his mind, he remembers the jealous rage that had distorted it, and the promise, delivered between clenched teeth, that he would be taught a lesson for daring to punch above his weight. Punch above his weight! Llyr groans again as he recalls something about Cerys and that he, Llyr, had tried to take advantage, and that piss-pots like him should be hung out to dry. Talking of being dry, why did he feel so wet Wincing he reaches down and with overwhelming shame finds that he's pissed himself. Oh God! He tries to sit up but his head spins alarmingly and he's overcome by such nausea he thinks he'll pass out.

Gingerly he lies back down and with one shuttered eye stares up at the grey drizzling sky and wishes himself dead.

He stays like that for some time as birdsong twitters about him and a tractor put-putters in some distant field. The air has grown chilly but he makes no effort to move, and with the constant thrum of pain as his companion, his defences come down and his thoughts drift to the sum of his life so far.

He is twenty-five years of age and has been living rough for over ten. The loss of his parents; wiped out by a driver so drunk that he couldn't even remember doing it, leaving Llyr, an only child of nine, all the angst of bereavement to deal with and no one to share it with. An orphan with no other family except for a distant cousin in New Zealand who had had no interest in the plight of his young relative; care for Llyr came courtesy of the 'System' although for him, it had been more akin to child abuse.

He'd been puny for his age, and with his disability, an easy target for the older, stronger children; and more often for the very people who were supposed to protect him. Having come from calm, loving home where he'd been an unexpected but very cherished surprise to older parents, the transition to a life of such casual brutality saw him run away again and again. But he was distinctive with his limping gait and he never got very far before the *Heddlu* picked him up. The last time he ran away he planned more carefully and left on a bus one day and to anonymity in the Midlands. There he stayed and survived the streets until adulthood, before drifting back to the place of his birth and then drifting about ever after.

It is a sad, sorry excuse for a life, he knows, but he had no high expectations of any other. Being beaten for begging or for just being 'different' was not unlike taking a fist for being good-looking. Or as his mother used to say, as fair of face as any Prince. For where he'd been deprived physically, the handsomeness of his features coupled with the distinctive intensity of his eyes was in stark contrast. Yet his natural good looks were frequently anything but a blessing and they often left him wide open to insults, jealousy and abuse. He was homeless and disabled and had no right to look like that! The world often judged harshly and liked to take umbrage when you didn't fit in. And sometimes, if you stuck out enough and failed to pass muster, you'd be sure to invite the kind of punishment that a bullying village lout like Dai Jenkins had decided to administer.

Llyr remembers the way he'd glowered at him the previous day, keen to show off his muscle and what action he could visit on a bloke half his size.

He never stood a chance. Like all the times before he'd just curled up like a ball and taken it. His crime on this occasion wasn't an off-look, the wrong look, getting in someone's way, or even just for the hell of it; the reason was for daring to accept kindness from a stranger who had shown him, in the eyes of his aggressor, favour that he coveted and wanted for his own. *And so this is the world I live in and the people whose paths I cross,* Llyr thought dully. *When would such things ever stop? What is the point of my life if all I'm ever going to be is a punch bag for other peoples' frustrations? How's about it if I just lie here and never get up again. Who would know, who, for that matter would even care?*

It isn't self-pity he's feeling; it's a weariness borne of years of struggle and being abused and as he lies damp, aching and bruised to the bone, he hears someone call his name. *Cerys...?*

Despite the roaring pain he manages to get himself on to his side, and gasping with the effort he tries to look about but the one eye that escaped the worst of the boot blurs everything into a haze.

"Cer... Cer..." he croaks but he can't get the word out. He thinks his jaw has been broken, such is the agony. But he rallies and with a blossoming hope in his heart, because suddenly he realises that he doesn't want to die alone in the woods like dog left for dead. Not this way. Not like this. Not with his pants full of piss and his body punched to a pulp. How would it be for Cerys to come back for her flask only to find his corpse! He wants to live! He needs help, medical help and he knows he needs it badly.

"Amb...amhulaaaaaa..." he mumbles. He can't form the words; his mouth won't let him. The pain in his jaw sears him into silence.

"Llyrrrrrr..." it's coming from the church.

With a huge effort Llyr gathers himself and begins to writhe his way forward like a snake trying to shed its skin. He hears his name again. It's definitely coming from inside the church. He strains his head to look and sees his bag still outside where he dropped it. The doors are both fully ajar and believing Cerys to be just beyond them he endures the bolts and flashes of pain and groaning with the effort keeps going. It takes everything he's got as his ears start to sing and oblivion threatens to take him. He's nearly there, just a few more feet! His breath is coming in awful gasps and every bone and muscle in his assaulted body protests volubly as slowly, agonisingly, he drags himself forward and then he's there.

At the threshold he slumps as he to tries to gain more breath into his tortured lungs, and then hands reach out and draw him in.

He must've blacked out again, he thinks, either that or he's dreaming because somehow he's back at the foot of the altar steps. Even though his vision's still blurry he can make out enough of the window to see that Jesus isn't moving this time, or even bothering to acknowledge him. He feels exhausted, detached, but aware enough to wonder how he made it this far. More importantly, where is Cerys? He tries to sit up and groans at the effort before succumbing to an almost unbearable pain. His head feel like a lump of deadweight that doesn't belong to him and his body as fragile as the finest porcelain.

"Ce... ys..." he mouths, it is little more than a distorted whisper and he feels an indescribable relief as a figure leans over him. And yet there is something different about her...

As poor and as fragmented as his vision in the one eye is, he sees enough to recognise that the hair is not the same; long, yes, but not light. And the clothes this woman/girl is wearing, of what he can see, are of a dark material; Cerys had a red hooded coat on, *unless she took it off,* he thinks dully, *or maybe my eye is so damaged I can't distinguish between colours anymore.*

He blinks with painful slowness and a hand appears before his face and makes a gentle sweep over it. He feels it like a soft breeze as it cools his brow. Almost immediately his vision begins to clear and he blinks more rapidly as the hazy lines of the woman sharpen and he sees that the hair is indeed fair, that she's wearing black, and that she isn't Cerys.

"Welcome back."

The smile she bestows on him is thin and coldly chilling, "My, my, you are in a bit of a mess, aren't you? I've taken the liberty of restoring some of the sight back in that eye. All the better for you to see, *and* remember me with, I hope…"

The smile becomes a leer and she lifts an eyebrow enquiringly as the dark eyes bore into him relentlessly, "And you *do* remember me, don't you? Llyyyyyyr…"

Like a gentle wave washing over him, the memory of her mysterious visit the previous night rises from some dark part of his mind and fills him with disquiet. He'd thought it to be a dream and had buried it along with all the other bits of mental debris he couldn't comprehend, but now he senses danger before him and can think only of one thing. Cerys.

"Your friend has gone. There's only you and I," the woman says as though reading his mind, "Shame she didn't stay around long enough to save you, but then, women can be *so* fickle, can they not!"

It was not a question that required an answer but Llyr felt a sudden urge to defend his absent but kindly Samaritan.

"Sh...Shu..." he winces with the effort and tails off; the pain indescribable.

The woman regards him coolly for a few moments and then her hand sweeps over him again, and this time it's stronger like a cold wind across his jaw. He stares up at her in wonder. The pain has gone completely. It's as though it had never been. Tentatively he moves his tongue around the inside of his mouth and explores the repaired damage. Even his teeth feel firmer.

"Better...?" Again that strange cold smile and he gives a small nod.

He regards her for some moments. There's something so different about her, alien almost; other-worldly

"Are you an angel?" he asks at last.

She throws back her head and laughs/barks in an odd parody of mirth and the sound smashes through his previous apathy as a cold finger of fear spikes the base of his spine and shoots through him like an electric shock. All of his primeval senses kick in and he feels something akin to a head rush as he realises that this woman is *far* from heavenly and that in his current state he is as vulnerable as a sitting duck – or a lamb to slaughter

He watches helplessly as her white hair ripples and her eyes flicker fire, and striations of strange colours chase themselves around her gown as all pretence of being anything other than what she is falls away. And she seems to grow taller, impossibly tall as her looming figure blocks out the light that bravely shines in through the robes of Jesus and his angels. She smiles down at him with a thinly-veiled air of satisfaction like the cat that has caught its quarry. And Llyr, with all the hopelessness that prey must feel when caught between the claws looks back in horror and feels the world slowly turn on its head.

"Sarah…" he breathes

"Oh, she died years ago," she said, "I'm Selinus now."

They study each other for several seconds before this strange creature seems to shrink back to her former size, and putting her head on one side she assumes an expression one could almost suggest was sympathetic. But her eyes are cold, having lightened to a sharp brittle blue, and Llyr shrank before them.

Gesturing at his broken form she says, "The price of love, it is a high one to pay, is it not? They would've done worse to me had I not escaped them. Much worse… and for what?"

Her hair moved around her ceaselessly as though seeking to give comfort and taking a strand she held it for a moment or two before letting it go.

"I was wronged – as you have been wronged. It was said that my sin was to be born with a passionate and wayward heart… but that wasn't the only thing I brought with me when I came into this world. And when those who sought my downfall learned of it, truly my fate was sealed for then they used it against me and to harry me to my death, and why? Because I was *different*!"

Thrusting both of her hands out she held them palms upwards with a fierce pride and cried. "These hands had *power!* The power of healing! And I, foolish girl that I was, sought only to do good with them. For what a greater gift could there be! And with them I would tend to ailing neighbours, soothe poor and sickly children, relieve all manner of aches and pains and give ease those on their final journey…"

The eyes flare a startling red before returning to a steady ice blue, and Llyr is fascinated despite the fear that races through him.

She has a macabre magnificence about her that brings to mind all of the bad queens and fairy witches he'd ever read of as a child. Only she's not a figure of fantasy frozen forever between the pages of a book. This character, whoever, whatever she is, is very much alive and with a very big axe to grind.

"And so they proclaimed to use my gift against me, for I had dared to look upon and love someone who was promised to another. *Dared*! For who was I, but a poor farmer's daughter! And my…"

She pauses and her eyes soften momentarily as the face took on a soft, wistful look that made her look almost human, "how beautiful I was… how beautiful and desirable and *irresistible* to the man who dared to love me back, and *oh how we loved!"*

And then her face darkens again and she spat so viciously he thought his heart would leap out of his chest.

"But that mealy-mouthed bitch of the minister couldn't let him go! Oh, no! She couldn't, she *wouldn't*, even when he begged to be released from his troth! Consumed with jealousy she drew on the only weapon left open to such a weak and needy wretch; she called me out as a *witch!*"

Fury is beginning to build around her with all the savagery of a storm, and Llyr wishes the stone slabbed floor would swallow him up as the creature once called Sarah recalls the injustices done to her like a vengeful snapping beast.

"A witch, I tell you, a *witch*! Destined for unimaginable torture and to die at the stake! Oh yes, once the finger was pointed and the charge was made, a death sentence then was passed on *me*! For *she*, aided by the Church and egged on by her father, would settle for nothing less and I was doomed to die and I knew it! But they reckoned without the passion of my wayward heart, and so I resolved I would take hold on my own destiny, and with it, the last and damning word."

She leans in close and her eyes narrow to icy slits and Llyr feels her breath like an ancient frost that prickles against his skin.

"I brought myself here, to this very place. And made good my demise for by then I cared not for my soul, or the consequences… so great was my *sin*!"

For just the merest second her eyes shift and a long-held misery looks out, before the ice clouds come over and in a thundering voice she cries.

"But what of *theirs!* They hounded me and harassed me and all but sent me to my death! I knew not to look for mercy nor appeal to the betterment of their *good, kind, Christian hearts!* And so I made a pact instead with a god who *welcomed* my differences and now you see me here before you as *he* made me!"

Her eyes blaze with white fire and she turns to glare into some corner of the church as her hair whips wildly about her head and the colours race and chase in fury around her gown.

"Come!" she bawls, and then with a wave of her hand Llyr is suddenly raised and suspended half reclining in the air as a mass of shadows uncoil towards him and he has an instant of sheer terror when he fears he will be given over to them. But as the witch steadies him he realises that she's raised him to a vantage point so he can see them better and he calms down. Overcome with curiosity he beholds them with his one good eye for he knows them for what they were. These are the lost souls Cerys had spoken about, the guilt-riddled ghosts, the sorrowful spirits earthbound with regret and cursed to wander forever.

The world around him has become increasingly surreal as events keep unfolding, and held tightly in the air by some unseen magic he can only watch fearfully as the shadowed forms cringe and cower before the woman they had once tormented. And Llyr surprises himself with how little pity he has for them. Indeed, he feels a twinge of sympathy and growing kinship with the white-haired woman who has been so badly wronged. And had she really been *so* bad? Hadn't she been driven to this state by the cruelty and prejudice of others when her only crime was to love a man and want to help people.

She had healed his jaw and his eye – but only one. Was she demonstrating her power to get him on side… or were her healing abilities limited? Something told him that there were more 'gifts' at her disposal than he'd care to speculate, and he gazes at her in awe and knows she could as easily smite him like a fly as heal his body whole, and sensing his scrutiny she lowers her voice to more measured tones, *reasonable* tones, and gestures towards the heaving mass.

"Llyr, you see before you the epitome of those who would play God, Judge, Jury and Executioner... and where did it get them? No further than the place in which they worshipped, and why was that? Because such was their *hypocrisy* neither side wanted them! And so here they all are, and have been, since causes more natural than my own took their lives, but not into the Light. Oh no..." she leers triumphantly, "And how they have yearned for it, called for it, *begged* for it, pleaded to be released from this state... and so I heard their cries, and asked that I may stake my claim. And *my* God... *my* Father deemed such a request *most* fitting and so they now belong to me! Ah, how the wheel spins and turns, eh."

She lunges towards her ghostly audience and there's a panicked flurry as they shrink back, "For you got more than you ever wished for when you came after Sarah Harris, didn't you! And now you know added misery as you so gave to me. And here they will stay and serve me until I decide what to do with them, for they may prove useful yet. Indeed, my Master..." she sweeps around to him, all honey-eyed, lips curling coyly, "has said we will need all the souls we can get if we are to succeed with our... *master plan!* And you would fit in perfectly, Llyr... indeed you would play such an important part, such an *essential* part, I'm not sure we would be able to do it without you..."

She flicks a hand at him and now Llyr looks out of two eyes for miraculously she has healed the other in an instant.

"This," she says, "is but a part of what I can do! What *he* can do! What *we* can do for you! For we can make you a *better* man, a *stronger* man, a more *powerful* man! A living, breathing, beautiful god! A god to rival all others!"

Her voice rises and resounds around the church as she towers like an avenging banshee.

"For have you not suffered! Have *we* not suffered, Llyr? And did you ask for your affliction? Had you asked to be *different*! To be derided, punished, and driven to despair!"

The very air trembles into silence as Llyr holds his breath. The lost souls quiver as an unseen ear listens and waits for his response. And then, with a contemptuous wave of her hand Selinus dismisses the lost souls and turns her attention back to Llyr. The fury has subsided. Her hair now gently waving. There is a soft curve about the lips and a sincerity in her voice that soothes as it caresses.

"Come with me, join with us, and we will heal all your woes… set yourself a destiny free of pain and dare to dream a better life…"

She touches his cheek with infinite tenderness and the chill of fear lifts from his heart.

"Why remain at the mercy of those who would mistreat you when a better path awaits? We'll protect and take care of you, and all physical imperfections will be," her hand moved delicately, "As though they had never been. For we would make of you *such* a man as has *never* been seen, and you, my *cariad*..." she nods slowly and the warmth of her eyes gleam with unbridled pleasure, "Would be *our* Messiah. *All-powerful, so* virile, almost *too* beautiful to behold such will be your... *perfection*! And all we ask of you, *all* that we request in return is your complete and willing surrender, your unquestioning obedience and desire to serve the Master."

The woman that was Sarah pauses to gauge the young man's reaction and is pleased to see that his soul is but a heartbeat away and her eyes flare like hot coals. Scenting victory, she goes in for the kill.

"Never again will you have to endure the indignities visited upon you as you have this day, Llyr. No more to be shunned, spurned and sent on your way. Indeed, those who would defile you will bow down before you, and they will ask, no, *beg* your forgiveness! And *you,* young man will have your day and more power than you ever thought possible!"

She holds out a hand as Llyr, still suspended, feels that he is on the knife edge of a decision that resonates with all he'd ever dreamt of, yearned for, wanted; and here it all is, laid out before him like some sumptuous banquet that he knows will destroy his taste buds forever, but the temptation is so strong and he feels his heart quicken. Her arguments were compelling. Would it be so bad?

But what if he said no? Would he be cast down and taken anyway? He was hardly in a position to put up much of a struggle. Or maybe, and more likely, he would be left in a heap, bruised and battered, to soak up whatever Fate had in store for him. He thought of Cerys coming to collect her flask and seeing him in this state, or worse. Or what if the village macho-man came back to finish the job, and here he'd be like a sacrificial sitting duck with no means of defence or escape.

His ribs ache incessantly and stab at him with every breath. Pulses of pain seep and flow and ebb and grow throughout his body and he feels so tired, so indescribably heavy.

He turns his head and looks up towards the man depicted in the faded stained glass and wonders what he would say to him now if he could speak. But Jesus doesn't turn his gaze nor move his lips in discourse. He looks out and beyond with that melancholy air as the angels' cluster around him frozen forever in their celestial dance.

He senses the eyes of the creature who had once been a woman steady upon him and the fear that had held him dissipates like a morning mist. The stench of his own urine lingers like a vaporous ghost and, amid the cracks and fissures of his mind, so nearly broken with the shame and humiliation of being unable to fight back, is the culmination of all he'd ever had to suffer and he takes the proffered hand.

There is a sharp intake of breath from Selinus, and Llyr feels an immediate pull and then a kind of subsidence within him, like something has been shifted, or taken. But the young man who was once a homeless wretch called Llyr, and named with love after a god of the sea, had no last moments of panic or regrets. Calmness overcomes him, a certainty of purpose that wraps around him and suffuses his whole being like a well-worn cloak. And as Selinus throws back her mane and crows her triumph, the fog lifts from his mind and he finds himself smiling. Not even the sight of the two huge wraiths that emerge from 'the maw' can diminish the strange pleasure he's feeling, and he's still smiling when they take him down.

## Chapter 6

Later that day Cerys sits across from her father and listens patiently as he gives, what he calls, a verbal cwtch. That translates, as she knows, as a gentle and yet probing conversation into what he deems worthy of fatherly concern, but Cerys affectionately regards them as nothing other than his tendency to worry and ensure all was okay in her world. Since the loss of her mother and her father's remarriage, their bond has remained strong and mutually supportive, and these chats were his means of reassurance; for both of them. Del and her mother are watching TV elsewhere in the house giving them space.

Sunday lunch is over but both remain sitting at the kitchen table with mugs of tea before them, at ease in each other's company despite the theme of conversation. It would appear that Mrs Jones had been prompt in reporting back. And Delyth, in revenge for having been found before she caught the bus no doubt, had also added her piece and between them had Cerys all but about to elope. Cerys sighs as her father laid bare the dangers of talking to strangers and how the perils of modern society were such that even living in the country was no guarantee of safety.

"Da," she says when he finished, "it was no big deal... yes, he was young, but no, I wasn't flirting!"

She suppresses a smile at this point, Mrs Jones and her imagination; not to mention her step-sister and her malicious mind!

"He fell down and I helped him. What else was I to do?" She spread her hands and raised her shoulders, her expression beguiling.

"You are a deacon of the chapel, da, what would you have done? Yes, exactly! You'd have done the same, and if Mrs Jones seen *that* she'd have been the first up to the pulpit to applaud you!"

Her father gives a slight frown but the brown eyes twinkle in the care-worn face.

"And as for Del! Da, you know how it is between me and her. She'd say anything if she thought it would knock my halo off!" she winks and her father smiles despite himself and pats her hand.

"Well as long as that's it, but..." he regards her levelly, his demeanour suddenly serious and Cerys knew immediately what was coming, "I thought I'd have some of my ham with eggs for breakfast, and well, as you don't eat meat, Cerys, I can only assume you're also feeding this young man. Where is he anyway?"

"Okay, I admit it; I took him some food early. He'd spent the night in the old church and I just wanted to check he was alright... I also borrowed your flask to take him some coffee."

"*Coffee!*" her father's brows disappear up into his hairline and Cerys laughs.

"Yes, da, *coffee!* Hardly a sin! Just some bread, ham, and coffee. You know yourself it was a cold start after all the lovely weather we've been having and I just..." she gives a small shrug, "wanted to be kind, I suppose. And I spoke with him, you know, and he really isn't bad or anything. Just a bit of a lost soul going nowhere in particular."

Now it was her father's turn to sigh, and he did so with a poor attempt at exasperation, "You'll need to get a tougher head. Never mind a heart, when you become a nurse, Cerys! You can't help everyone who's down on their luck or else you'll be costing me a fortune in flasks!"

The twinkle was back and rising suddenly Cerys went over to him and threw her arms around his neck.

"I should've known nothing gets by you, da, and I will bring your flask back, I promise. Llyr said he'd be moving on today so our paths will probably never cross again anyway."

"Llyr?" he says pulling back from her embrace. "Cerys, just promise me you'll be more careful in future, will you? It's one thing to help a stranger, quite another to go off and visit them! *Iesu Grist,* anything could've happened!"

"But it didn't and..."

She caught sight of his worried face and broke off, planting a kiss on his cheek instead.

"Yes, you're right, and I'm sorry, da."

He took her face in his hands and the soft brown eyes were poignant.

"You're all I have left of your mam, cariad, and that makes you all the more precious for that. So no more visiting strange men, young or otherwise, in old churches... promise?"

"I promise."

He hugged her to him.

"Right then, now that's settled we'd best go and join Cat and Delyth, and as for the flask – don't worry about it, Cerys. Your wandering friend has probably taken it with him."

She made no reply. But as they retired to the living room and the blaring TV, Cerys had the thought that she'd slip along to the church later and retrieve the flask. It would show her da that she had good judgement, that she wasn't his little girl anymore, and besides, Llyr would be well on the road by then, so where would be the harm.

Meanwhile just a few doors down across the village street, Dai stretched out along the length of sofa, as his da snoozed in his favourite chair and his mam, as usual, was pottering around in the kitchen. For someone who had achieved very little in his life he truly believes he's made huge inroads this day. And as some afternoon soap babbles away on the big-screen TV, his mind is elsewhere, far elsewhere.

With pleasure he recalls the look on the boyo's face as he came out of the church fumbling at his crotch – fantasising about Cerys, no doubt! The sudden moment of shock as he saw Dai looming up before him and how easily he went down with the first punch. Dai hadn't meant to go so far, of course, but it was hard not to when the rage came upon him, and seeing the recipient of his anger groaning in the grass had incensed him to new heights. It wasn't until he saw the tell-tale signs of piss darkening the grubby trousers that he reined himself in with the thought that perhaps he'd done enough.

He smiled. He'd done enough alright. Left that low-life motionless and stinking in the grass like the piece of shit he was! He wondered how Cerys would like her pretty boy now. Sat in the church drinking coffee like they were on some kind of a date! He ruminated with disgust. Just wait until he told the boys! Just a small reminder that you didn't mess with Dafydd Jenkins!

But no word of what he'd done must reach the ears of Cerys – or else he could kiss any chance with her goodbye! He stirred, as he always did, at the thought of her. God, but she was her own woman! Sometimes he thought maybe it was because she made herself so inaccessible to him that drove him mad with his need for her. But one thing was for sure, he told himself, that runty git won't be back in these parts in a hurry, and besides, he was doing the village a favour! Nobody wanted some low-life like that hanging around and claiming false charity. People like that belonged in the cities. He gave another smile, smugly content in his reasoning. Yes, if anything he'd performed a public service! And one day perhaps, when Cerys came to her senses and saw him for the good guy he really was, he might even tell her what he'd done – just to prove how much he cared.

Cerys didn't make it back to the church that evening. The drizzle had turned to a steady downpour so she turned her attention to the paperwork needed for her college enrolment instead. Term would be starting soon, and filled with the excitement of fulfilling her dream Cerys attended to the necessary preparations and it was a couple of days later when she realised she still hadn't retrieved the flask.

The recent wet weather had given way to long, grey, drizzly days and, thinking she'd better get a move on before she completely forgot, she took her red hooded mac from the hall as Delyth came sidling down the stairs.

"Where are you off?" she all but demanded.

"Out." said Cerys shortly.

Things with her stepsister had been more touchy than usual the past couple of days. Delyth was still holding a grudge for, as she put it, Cerys ruining her last day of the heat wave. But with more important things on her mind, Cerys found it necessary and far easier to be brief in her dealings with her stepsister and now was no exception.

"Yes, I know that – but where 'out'!"

"Del, I'd no sooner tell you my business than I would go out with Dai Jenkins!" Cerys pulled the zip up and then turning to Delyth she wagged a finger warningly saying, "And don't think I've forgotten about you stirring the pot with him the other day..."

Delyth giggled, "You should have seen his face! He went so red I thought his head was going to pop off! He's got it bad for you, though, Cerys – he all but follows you 'round the village with his tongue hanging out!"

"No, he does not!" But Cerys laughed in spite of herself, and they grinned at each other in a rare moment of accord.

"You could do worse. It's not like he's too ugly or anything."

Cerys pretended to be outraged, "Do worse? He's practically a Neanderthal, Delyth!"

"So if you're not meeting him – then where *are* you going?"

"Nice try, Del, but still I'm not telling!"

"Ah well," said Delyth with a swift return to her usual tartness, "if you're not going to tell me then I'm hardly going to lose any sleep over it, am I! Best you run along, then, Princess Precious."

Cerys shook her head and smiled at the retreating back. It was a shame they didn't get along – or more to the point, that Del refused to. They could, if they really put their minds to it, and have a lot of fun, actually do things together. Maybe one day, when Delyth comes out of her 'teenage phase' as Cerys saw it. But she wouldn't be holding her breath anytime soon.

Despite the dreariness of the day, Cerys stepped out smartly and making her way along the village street she espied three figures huddled around the door of the Jenkins house. They saw her, too, and fell into silence as they watched her progress. Dai holding court with his cronies, thought Cerys dismissively, and waved a vague hand unwilling to engage any further.

As soon as she was past Neil spluttered and turned mischievous eyes on Dai's discomfiture.

"Bloody hell, talk of the devil!" he chortled and ducked as Dai aimed a playful cuff, "Although, to be fair, I think *angel* would be a better word to describe Cerys! You on the other hand, Dafydd Jenkins, would most definitely take the crown for Old Nick. Bloody hell, but she'd have a fit, if she knew!"

"All the more reason to keep your mouth shut!" Dai glowered warningly.

"Oh don't sweat it, mun!" said Neil, "She won't hear anything from us! Wonder where she's off, though – you don't think she's going back to check on him, do you?"

"Nah," Dai shifted position as he leaned against the door frame, "probably getting the bus. Besides, I reckon pretty-boy will be long gone – once he'd changed out of his bundies!"

They all sniggered, careful to keep their voices low but all thoroughly enjoying the intrigue.

"Sounds as though you gave him a good pasting, mind, Dai," Twm said admiringly, "maybe he's still there. Are you sure you left him breathing, never mind in any state to walk?!"

"His kind always finds a way to walk – even if they crawl along their belly!" Dai retorted with contempt and missed the bemused look that passed between his friends. "He was sniffing 'round, playing the sympathy card and I wasn't having it, I'm telling you! Anyway I heard them talking as she was leaving, and as far as she was concerned he was going."

His jaw jutted aggressively, the pale eyes taking on an icy glint, "And if I find anyone messing 'round with that girl, or *even thinking* of trying their luck! Believe me, I'll make what I did to him look like a clip 'round the ear..."

He glared out across the street and his two best friends, well-versed in the world according to Dai Jenkins Junior, had no doubt of it and nodded their heads vigorously.

Cerys hurried through the woods her mind busy with plans to meet up with friends later. It would be her last chance to really let her hair down before knuckling down to some serious study, and in her usual enthusiasm she inwardly embraced both. As she came into the clearing she caught sight of Llyr's bag outside the church and stopped dead in her tracks. And it was his bag; she had no doubt of that. But where was he? Perplexed she looked about

"Llyr?" she called tentatively, and then more strongly, "Hello... anyone...?"

A hush descended over the woods and even the birds ceased in their twittering as though to listen. Cerys turned around slowly on the spot, eyes searching the dripping foliage, ears finely tuned for an answering voice. But there was nothing, just a heavy silence, and fleetingly she thought of the stories associated with this place and suppressed a shiver. She glanced again at the bag. Yes, it was definitely his. A dark blue luggage bag, voluminous and packed to the hilt with whatever precious possessions he owned.

"*Llyr!*" her voice more urgent now as the idea of someone, anyone, leaving their whole world behind in an over-stuffed bag was as incomprehensible to her as it was odd. Silence continued to reign as she felt the first pangs of concern. Could this be a trap? Had her father been right all along? Had she allowed her softness to get in the way of common sense leaving herself wide open to ... what?

Taking a firm hold of herself she called again.

"LLYR!"

Only this time her tone was more strident, confident. But still there was no answering call, and determined not to allow her imagination run away from what could well be a perfectly reasonable explanation, she strode forward towards the church doors only to find them shut firmly against her.

Bloody hell, what was going on! Annoyance had now replaced the first inklings of fear and she shoved against them hard and was pleasantly surprised at the ease with which they opened before her.

She peeked in. "Llyr...?"

As usual the church was dark and dismal and there was nothing to see other than Jesus with his angels and the cracked altar stone. There was no sign of Llyr so she could only suppose he was somewhere close by, or perhaps he'd got spooked and made a painful run from whatever it was that had frightened him. For right now, that was the only explanation her mind could come up with, and she stepped inside hoping her faith would be justified in him and that she would find the flask.

And there it was! Left just as she had requested behind one of the doors. She retrieved it with a happy sense of relief and it was only as she came back out that she saw Llyr's bag and thought maybe she should move it inside.

She paused as she considered it. On the one hand it wasn't her problem; who was to say he'd come back? But then, what if he did when he'd calmed down, and everything he owned was still sat out in the penetrable damp doing Lord knows what damage?

She tutted to herself and without further ado, grabbed one of the handles and heaved it in past the doors and then into a corner thinking, he'll see it there – if he comes back. The church would be the first place he'd check, surely, and just as she was about to leave she heard a voice.

She froze. There was no one else in the church, she would swear to it and yet someone had just called her name and she knew she hadn't imagined it...

It came again, out of the dimness of the inner church and *behind* her.

"Cerys..."

Spoken with such gentle tenderness she felt the hairs stand to attention at the back of her neck, and there was also something about the voice that was strangely familiar and yet... Petrified to the spot, every fibre of her being cried out to *run, move, do something!* But she was like a frightened deer caught in mid-flight, and only her eyes moved as they darted about as the voice came again behind her. Closer this time...

"Cerys. Don't be afraid."

There was an innate kindness in the voice. A softness that soothed as it reassured, and it drew at her deeply as the moon does the tides of the sea, and as she found herself turning as the voice coaxed further, she moved with an agonising slowness as though in a dream, and as she came around and her eyes found the source; the air stopped in her lungs as her heart skipped a beat, and her mouth fell open as the world took a spin, and finding no words, she dropped her father's flask with a clatter before falling to her knees.

## Chapter 7

The man who stood before her she had seen many, many times before; in books, in films, in religious pamphlets and now amazingly, incredibly, unbelievably, in the flesh. And indeed he looked as he was often depicted and yes, she felt that she knew him in her eyes and in her heart as surely she knew her own father. Tears teased her eyes and threatened a deluge, so great was the moment, and on her knees she remained oblivious to the cold, stone floor, because here, stood before her, was the Son of God himself.

He smiled at her, so much love, so much beauty and just in the eyes themselves. They radiated power and enigma as old as Time itself, and caught up in the depths of the most exquisite sea-green, Cerys forgot to breathe and just stared and stared, stricken mute and euphoric by the presence in which she found herself in.

Bending down the figure took her hands and with infinite tenderness drew her to her feet. All the while his gaze never left hers, and as Cerys found her feet beneath her, so weak were her legs, she felt sure they wouldn't be able to hold her and that she'd simply crumple and see-saw down to the ground like pieces of delicate paper.

"Cerys," the voice was low, gentle, musical and soft with compassion, "Be not afraid of me, I tell thee, be not afraid."

To see His face so close with the neatly trimmed beard and the warm olive skin rendered any words Cerys chose to emit, useless. Oh my God, but he was *so* beautiful, *so* full of love, so *divine*. She remembered to breathe and took great ragged breaths as gradually she became aware of the birds singing outside, and her world – the world that she knew and was so familiar with, began slowly to settle back into place and she blinked several times before it dawned on her that this was actually happening.

"My Lord..." she breathed in wonder.

She had never been particularly religious, despite the best attempts of her father and early years at the chapel, and yet here was the unmistakeable proof and her heart soared like a bird and squeezed painfully in turn.

"Can it really be? How can you... can this..." her voice trailed off, overwhelmed by the enormity of what was happening, and she shuddered with a frisson of pleasure as he placed a warm finger to her lips.

"My dearest child, do you doubt your own eyes? Have you no reckoning of how great the power of my Father is as to forsake all that would be deemed impossible?" There was just the merest hint of rebuke in the tone and Cerys flushed a deep scarlet.

"Oh, no! No, no, my Lord! I did not mean to question, I swear, I... I..." on the verge of tears of a different kind now she paused mortified into silence and he shushed her as gently as you would a whimpering baby.

"Oh my poor, dear child, do not be troubled... my presence is of such great magnitude it almost too much to bear, this I understand... but you must trust what you feel in your heart for I am who you see, and who you perceive me to be. I am Jesus, the Son of God."

Cerys went to drop to her knees again but by the strength of His hands and sheer force of will, he indicated that she was to remain standing.

"Let there be no kneeling to me, Cerys, not from you," he smiled knowingly and for one incongruous moment Cerys thought he was about to wink, "mine very own and most beloved Good Samaritan..."

He raised His perfect eyebrows and she felt her mouth fall open.

What was this he was saying, *implying*? *Beloved Good Samaritan*? *Llyr*? No! Surely not! Surely it could not be! Llyr the homeless man, Llyr the cripple, Llyr with whom she'd sat and drank coffee with *right here* in this very church!

Her mind was in a spin! But then could this be why she had felt so drawn to him, so *safe*! Why she'd gone above and beyond to the point of seeking him out the very next morning, all of that for an *ordinary man?* Or was it because she sensed a greater being, a *special* being beneath the lonely soul of the road that *he* had been guided to *her!*

And those eyes, his eyes, *these* eyes were all but one and the same, and the way he smiled, the handsome cast of his features, the strange attraction she had felt... was *feeling.* She pulled back. Confused by what she could only regard as an inappropriate thought, her mind continued to spin and her heart still raced as she strived to find some semblance of self and understanding of the situation.

Jesus regarded her gravely but with a hint of bemusement that led her to believe he had read her thoughts. She looked down and away from his appraisal and felt the heat rising in her cheeks. Her thoughts were in complete disarray. He couldn't be suggesting. He wasn't really saying, is he really saying that...

"Cerys," he said solemnly and he lifted her chin, "I know this has all come as a bit of a shock, but you must have heard of the saying that angels come in many guises... Well, hear me when I tell you, that so have I, the Son of God."

She looked into his eyes and saw only truth and an earnest sincerity in the sea-green depths.

"Think not that because of who you are, and the humbleness of where we are in some way lessens the moment... Why the deserts of the Holy Land when the precincts of this ancient church in an ancient land will do just as well..." He left the question hanging in the air like an unfinished dream and went on.

"I have come, as you see me, as quiet as a mouse in the dark of night for I would have no roar to announce me," he paused, "and nor would I put myself at the mercy of they who would as soon destroy me as cast me in a cage. For modern man has advanced no further since I walked to my death in Jerusalem, and hear me when I say; there will be no cross for me this time."

Cerys stared at him with eyes grown huge and saw emerald chips in the depths of his, and her skin prickled as it came to her suddenly that this was not the kindly, turn-the-other-cheek kind of Jesus that walked Galilee back in the day. This was a tougher, shrewd, more resilient Jesus – a *dangerous* Jesus!

Inwardly she caught at herself. Where were these thoughts coming from? Why was she *thinking* all of these things so inherently blasphemous! Her head began to ache, a dull nagging that picked and chivvied. It all just seemed *too much*! And as her mind teetered precariously on the edge of a dark abyss, she reached out blindly for something, anything to hang on to and the thought came to her like a ray of light. Eagerly she grabbed out at it and held on tight. Mam…

"Mam! My mam! Is she with you in heaven? Is she *there?"*

Just hearing her voice and asking the question was enough to calm the turbulent seas within and she drew a deep breath as she waited, her whole being bristling with anticipation.

The green eyes glowed and again the hand lifted from hers and stroked her face lovingly, "Your mother dwells amongst us in the Kingdom of Heaven, Cerys. And know that she is at peace with my Father and keeps company with his angels, and know that even now she looks down upon us and with blessings for you, her only daughter," Again the beautiful smile, "For she is as proud to have borne you into this world as she now watches over you from another. And with no less love, indeed her love now even greater for your tender care of me…"

The tears that had been held in abeyance found release and came pouring down as the man who called himself Jesus wrapped her in his arms and cradled her until the weeping stopped. Cerys trembled with all manner of emotions; reverence, elation, disbelief, and a wild but fettered joy. Could this really be happening! To be in the arms of Jesus Christ himself? To feel the warmth of his cheek on her head, to hear that holy heart beating against hers? And his robes, so soft and of the purest white and with just a hint of other-world seasons, sunshine and spices.

She stays still against him until the tears are gone and she takes the first real comfort she had ever truly known since her mother was taken.

Cerys always thought of her mam's demise as having been 'taken' over all the other platitudes that were doled out for death and dying. Her mam, her beautiful mam, so kind, so full of life. Struck down and sentenced by the very fate of those she had nursed to the end. And the cancer that took hold of her was so aggressive, so virulent, that she was gone (taken) within six months. Such a cruel and twisted end for someone who had devoted her life to providing care to those in the final twilight of theirs.

And it was through the legacy of this that Cerys had set herself on the path to be a nurse in palliative care like her mother. It seemed a fitting tribute and would act as a balm to her grief. And now, it seemed most fitting in Cerys' eyes that her mam now kept company with angels, and she sighed as an exquisite sense of profound peace stole over her.

Now that the storm has passed, Jesus tenderly extricates her from his embrace but keeps her hands in his. He fixes her with an intent look.

"Now child, there is something I would ask of you, indeed I would *beseech* that you heed me well. My presence here must not be discovered nor made common knowledge. Nobody can know I am here. Not now. Not yet. I am trusting you to hold my confidence as close to your heart as if it were your own. Cerys can you give me your word and promise me you will say nothing?"

She gazes deeply into pools of liquid love and there is no hesitation.

"I give you my word."

She was beginning to feel much calmer as though drifting along in a dream-like state. But it was a good dream-like state, and she wished she could remain folded in his arms forever. She was caught up, smitten, suffused and completely enslaved by the moment and the man. For here was the Son of God, not only revealing himself to her, but beseeching her, (*Beseeching!* Her!) To keep a secret! To share a secret! To be part of the most miraculous event since this man rose from the tomb over two thousand years before! Her profound gratitude and sense of awe that she should be a part of this was as humbling as it was extraordinary and giving in to an urge to reassure him further, she adds passionately,

"My Lord, I would rather lay down my life than betray your confidence in me and I promise you, *I swear on* the soul of my mam in heaven that I will not breathe a word to anyone!"

He smiles graciously and squeezes her hands gently, and Cerys, emboldened by a belief that a bond has been set, dares to ask the ultimate question that has been bothering her.

"My Lord, forgive me, but I must ask. You called me your very own Good Samaritan. Does that mean that *you* were the man that I met on the road that day called Llyr? Was it really, truly you as... *him?*"

"Yes, child. I was that man. Only I was not he and he was not I. But by assuming the identity of another thus was I able to fulfil a greater purpose all of which..." and again he placed a finger over Cerys's lips, "Will be revealed in good time."

Holding her fast with the beauty of that sea-green stare he went on.

"But I will tell you this; I am the true Man, the Son and the Holy Spirit. And you, Cerys, have been chosen for the very kindness that so marked your mother. A rare and noble trait that has favoured you in my Father's eyes. You have been selected for a great honour and so will you be rewarded, and believe me when I tell you."

He leaned in and with a low and vibrant intensity he added, "Not all rewards come to those in heaven... keep me hidden and my presence unknown, and you will know such blessings as can only be dreamed of..."

Her mind reels and a flush of something deep and primeval thrills through her, and in that very moment if he had asked her to throw herself off the roof she would have done it.

He releases her hands suddenly and glancing towards the doors says, "Leave now before you are missed, but come again tomorrow and we will speak more. And remember, my child, not a word to anyone."

She is reluctant to leave, but recognises the sense of what he was saying, and dashing the remains of the tears from her face, she takes a deep breath and nods. Still feeling incredibly surreal she turns and makes for the doors, and as she comes to the threshold she pauses and looks back.

And there he still is, the symbol of all Christian hopes and dreams; the man who died and rose again; a Saviour and the Son of God; no more a myth embodied forever in countless tracts and endless images – this was the *real* thing, the *real* man. The actual Son of God. And here was she; Cerys Watkins, an ordinary Welsh girl from an ordinary Welsh village and the only one in the whole wide world right who knew and her heart sang with the magic of it, and then she turned and left the church.

*Clap, clap, clap!*

"Bravo! *Bravo!*" The man who was once called Llyr spun around as Selinus sways towards him. Her face is inflamed with excitement, her eyes blistering with a wild glee as she claps again and comes to stand before the white-robed figure.

"My! But you are a sight to behold and what words! *What words*! And such presence, *my Lord,* such *charisma!* You nearly had me fooled! A brilliant performance, truly outstanding!" she beams, "By the power of Satan, no one would doubt you're not the true Messiah, why, even the Master believes you have surpassed *all* expectations and you have pleased him well. Therefore, a reward he has in mind for you, but such a reward as will make the angels weep and set you on a path to greatness..." her orange eyes slant and her smile becomes salacious.

"We know you harbour feelings for that girl. As we also know that you have never known a woman carnally, and *that* makes you exceptional in the scheme of what my Master has planned. The girl, also, is untouched, yet she is not averse to the pull of desire nor the effect you are having on her – and so why not have her ... have her, Llyr, *take her* with our blessing."

Selinus leans in and places a hand on his arm.

"There is no end to the possibilities that lie before you and we'll move hell and earth to make it happen, I assure you. The Master has foreseen a new destiny for you, Llyr, for he believes that in this modern world a man should be allowed to enjoy his pleasures and live according to the desires of the flesh. And so he bids that you woo her, win her, and bring her over to us... and then..."

Again the sly look and she flicks her tongue across her thin lips like a snake, "The potency of such innocence combined will truly make such a pact that not even God himself will be able to pull it asunder!"

## Chapter 8

Cerys came out of the church and ambled slowly through the clearing to the path in the woods, oblivious to everything around her. To think, as she had been making her way in how her thoughts had been filled an evening planned with friends and gossip. A bite to eat and perhaps some wine thrown in; but there would be no evening out now. Her mind was too full, too preoccupied. Too *thrilled* to even consider sitting down and talking boys and college when she had just spoken with the King of Kings! And what of her mother!

Her much-missed and beloved mam. *Oh mam!*

Cerys's heart swelled at the memory of what he had said; happy and with the angels! Oh, but how a part of her wished she could rush home and tell her father, but she was under strict instruction and had sworn an oath. And one did not break one's word to the Son of God. The very idea was unthinkable!

For once in her life she'd been the recipient of another man's authority that was not her fathers, and as emotionally charged and as overwhelmed as she was, she knew she would keep his secret. Oh but what a secret... And that she, Cerys Watkins of Ty Gwyn cottage had been chosen to keep it! And all because of a random act of kindness – or was it? Was it possible that the whole scenario had been planned and pre-ordained? He'd hinted at such, and that she'd been selected, in which case... her mind was so busy she came out of the woods and nearly bumped into old Mrs Jones who was tottering past with her trolley.

The old lady glared as Cerys mumbled an apology, and then seeing her face tear-stained and distracted her annoyance gave way to concern.

"Why, Cerys, bach, have you been crying?"

Like magic Mrs Jones produced a neatly folded hanky and began to dab at Cerys's face, "There, there, cariad, come now, tell me what's made you sad? Has something happened?"

Mrs Jones was a canny old soul and glanced down the path to the woods and pursed her lips. Some secret assignation that had gone awry perhaps or something worse, much worse...

"Cerys, bach, what is it, I wish you'd tell me, what's happened?"

"Oh Mrs Jones," said Cerys trying to fend off her attentions with the hanky, "it's nothing... I'm fine, honestly! I just went for a walk and got to thinking about my mam, is all."

She felt bad lying to this old stalwart of the village, but then she hadn't been lying exactly, she *had* been thinking about her mother, and of all the people to bump into in her present state...

"Oh *bechod,* come on, then," the old lady said briskly and put her arm through Cerys', "I'll walk you home, or perhaps you'd like to come to mine for a *panad,* the shopping can wait."

"No, no, it's alright, Mrs Jones. Please don't make a fuss!"

Seeing the hurt expression flitter over the older woman's face Cerys immediately felt contrite but the last thing she needed was an escort back to the house and the inevitable questioning. With great care she extricated her arm and forced a smile to her face that she hoped looked convincing.

"Thank you, Mrs Jones, really. You're very kind, but I just need to be alone. I'll be fine, I promise. Please, don't miss the bus because of me."

"Well, if you are sure…"

"Yes, yes, I am. But thanks again anyway, Mrs Jones."

Mrs Jones studied her for a moment and seemed appeased enough for her to give a quick nod before rattling her way over to the bus stop. This was going to be hard, thought Cerys, *extremely* hard, and maybe the sooner she went home the better before she drew any more unwanted attention to herself.

As she opened the front door and entered the hall she was met with raised voices and it didn't take long to work out whose: Del and her mam. Again! But what better way to come back into the real world than walking into the usual mother and daughter battle for supremacy and for the first time in the last hour or so felt some modicum of normality.

"I said, no, and that's my last word!"

"Oh mam, that's so unfair!" Delyth came stomping out of the kitchen her face like thunder and pushed past Cerys before slamming her way out of the house. Catrin stepped out into the hallway looking equally harassed, and seeing her step-daughter made a gesture of despair.

"I don't know. That girl! I swear her behaviour gets worse not better! Wants to go to the cinema with her friends and a takeaway afterwards! Must think we're made of money! Good job your father isn't here, he so hates these scenes..." She broke off and looked at Cerys closely, "Are you alright, cariad, you look a bit peaky. Have you been crying?"

"Just a headache, Cat, I'll be alright in a bit. Think I'll go and have a lie down though."

As Cerys turned for the stairs her stepmother reached out and put a hand on her arm.

"I'm sorry you had to come in on that, Cerys. I know things are not easy with Del and that it must be really difficult for you at times. But things will hopefully get better once you're in college and away from the histrionics. Think she'll calm down a bit then, maybe get her life in order and, well, we can hope!"

The blue eyes were filled with genuine concern. Cerys often felt lucky that her father had chosen such a *nice* woman as his next wife, and Catrin was never anything but unfailingly kind to Cerys, giving rise to the family joke that Delyth must've been swapped at birth.

Cerys smiled and Catrin gently squeezed her arm, "Fancy a cup of tea? I'll bring it up if you like. You really do look quite pale, *cariad*. I hope you're not coming down with anything."

She laid a cool palm against her brow and frowned slightly, "You do feel a bit hot actually. Aren't you supposed to be meeting up with your friends later?"

"I'm going to cancel, think I'll have a quiet night in instead. But thanks, Catrin, a cup of tea would be lovely."

"Consider it done! You go on up to your room and I'll be there now in a minute."

Cerys sent a message to all of her friends as soon as she was alone using her headache as the means to cry off from the evening. And her head was aching. All she wanted was to be alone. To think, mull over things, and think some more. She still felt slightly at odds with the world, but better in herself and it felt good to be in her own room. Her stepmother gave a small tap on the door and came in with a small tray. She had brought tablets with the tea and a glass of water.

"I've also brought you a couple of digestives to line your stomach, cariad. Must do these things properly!" she said smilingly and Cerys thanked her.

The tablets remained untouched as did the biscuits, but Cerys drank the tea and then stretched out feeling inordinately sleepy. All of the thoughts that had been doing a steady jog around her head began to slow down becoming an amble before stopping altogether and she relaxed gladly into the first stages of sleep. As she drifted off she saw again in her mind's eye those beautiful green eyes and something stirred deep within her heart.

Sometime later she was awoken by a tap on the door and raising herself up on one elbow she called, "Come in."

It was her father and he came tentatively in and sat at the end of the bed as Cerys drew herself up yawning. She couldn't remember the last time she'd taken a nap in the day.

"How are you, *bach*? Catrin said you weren't feeling very well and have cancelled your cackle night with the girls. Are you feeling any better?"

His gentle face, so full of love pulled at her heart and she threw herself into his arms.

"Oh da!"

"Why, what is it, cariad, what's wrong?"

He was slightly bewildered at this sudden display of unprecedented emotion. Cerys wasn't usually quite so...*child-like!* That was more Delyth's department, he thought ruefully.

But Cerys was feeling passion in this moment. A great surge of love for this wonderfully kind man who was her da and who doted on her. And whose pain at the loss of her mother she knew she could assuage in an instant, and yet she could not, and the conflict rose up in her and she trembled in a state of flux between extreme joy and troubled confusion.

"Is it mam, *bach*...?"

The question was asked carefully, for her father couldn't think of anything else that would elicit such behaviour, and his relief was oddly reassuring as he felt Cerys nod against him. He cwtched her against him closely and said, "You're going to have moments like this, *cariad*, when the pain of losing her will rise up suddenly and take you off-guard...it's all part of the healing process; or so it's said...but we'll never forget her and we'll always love her, and I know how proud she would be to know you're all set for college and will be following in her footsteps, Cerys... Extremely *proud!* As am I."

Cerys pulled back and they regarded each other solemnly, and she wished she could tell him what she'd learned about mam. It pulled at her like powerful magnet for she rarely held secrets from her father. Their relationship was such that they were at ease with most things and each other since mam had gone. And it had just been the two of them for several years before Catrin and her daughter came along.

"And I'll do my best. I'll always try to do my best, no matter what. And you know that. Don't you, da...?"

"What's this? Of course I do!" he looked at her searchingly, "What a strange thing to say, Cerys. Are you sure there isn't anything else bothering you, my cariad? Has Delyth said something?"

She shook her head but he knew his daughter well enough to know that something was troubling her and his mind floundered for possible causes. But being such an uncomplicated man rarely plagued by dubious delights of a fervent imagination, he could think of nothing else other than it being the ever-burgeoning burden of bereavement, and leaned forward and he kissed the top of her head.

"You are so precious to me. And you know you can tell me *anything*, Cerys, *anything!* I am always here for you. Always here and ready to listen. Now then! How's about some tea, eh? I believe your favourite dish is currently being cooked in the oven." his smile was bright and brave and he cocked an eyebrow enquiringly, "which means we'll all be veggie tonight, and if that doesn't cheer you up then I don't know what will. Delyth hates quorn!"

He winked and Cerys giggled and the mood was broken.

"There, see! There's always someone worse off than us, so as you won't be seeing your friends tonight – let's at least try and have a pleasant evening and we may yet live dangerously and get the Scrabble out later!"

For the next several days Cerys made further visits to the church. She wouldn't stay long, maybe an hour at most, and she took great care to keep her movement's hidden, visiting at different times. But of course living in such a tiny village, it was practically impossible to keep anyone's movements a secret, but Cerys did as best as she could to appear normal. It would seem, as yet, that Mrs Jones had held her peace after their encounter the other day and Cerys was hugely grateful for that. There was one individual, however, who was taking particular interest in her comings and, goings, and as Dai Jenkins had been laid low by a heavy cold he could only watch from his window and speculate the reason as he sniffed and sneezed feeling sorry for himself.

It was hard for Cerys to maintain an interest in anything other than the real life miracle she visited every day. And although she assumed he came and went at will, he was always there calmly waiting for her. Resplendent in his white robes and an aura of aesthetic brilliance, he took her breath away every time. And the touch of his hands when he held hers! The warmth and the love, the trust, the *feeling!*

Cerys had not attended chapel for many years. Not since her mam was taken and her father, in his wisdom, thought it best not to press her. Yet he, as a regular worshipper and one of the pillars of the chapel community, had thrown himself into prayer and study, helped greatly by the local minister, Huw Powell, who had lost his wife some years ago and so knew well the pain.

Her lack of religious commitment, however, did not seem to matter nor have any bearing on the situation she found herself in, and when downcast with guilt she had raised it one day as a matter of concern, Jesus was quick to sweep her worries away.

"It is because you are not that is the reason you were chosen, Cerys. You are like an open vessel through which truth and purity runs clearly. I ask you; how many people who worship my God, the Father would have turned their faces away when Llyr stumbled and fell at the road side? How many would have sullied their hands reaching down to help a *poor* man less fortunate than themselves and lifted him up? Very few, I tell can tell thee. So concern yourself not with the falseness of faith and know that it is what is in the heart that counts."

She loved hearing him speak, how he'd alternate between archaic speech one minute and modern the next. And as she gradually adjusted to this most extraordinary situation it became difficult not to ask questions; and Lord knows she had many. But her reverence of respect dictated that this was no ordinary man with whom to badger questions with, but sometimes the urge to do so was so strong it became well-nigh unbearable. She needed, wanted, *had* to know so many things – and of course she yearned to learn more of her mother, but there was a shift in the energy around Jesus when her curiosity got the better of her, and sensitive to every nuance and change in this man, she'd cringe from the question knowing she'd gone too far.

What seemed incredible was that he seemed to be extremely interested in *her!* Much of the time they spent together involved talking about her hopes, aspirations, and how she would like her life to be. At times she found it bizarre and not a little unsettling at the turns some of these conversations would take; and if she didn't know any better she would almost swear at times that he actually appeared to be flirting with her!

The idea was as unrealistic as it was ridiculous, but there had been moments, like the way he looked at her sometimes, or brushed his fingers across her hand, the way he'd smile and watch her shudder. And as sinful and as inappropriate as she knew her thoughts to be; they came to haunt her regularly, waking her in the middle of the night, filling her head with impossible scenarios, and she rolled ceaselessly in her confusion between bouts of ecstasy and shameful self-reproach.

And as time went on, this burden, too prodigious for such young shoulders began to colour her behaviour and she stopped texting friends, and spent more and more time alone in her room. Her appetite, usually so voracious became picky and apathetic and those closest to her couldn't help but notice the difference. Her father asked her on more than one occasion if there was anything bothering her, and she'd catch her stepmother eyeing her at odd moments. Delyth was currently ignoring her which in some ways made things easier, but Cerys had withdrawn so much from the world that even college, which was starting in a week's time, failed to instil any interest and it was only during her time at the church when she was with *him* that she truly felt alive. And as soon as she left the warm glow of his presence, the rest of the world became a drab, grey place, and she'd walk home slowly with her chin on her chest.

Dai Jenkins, with nothing better to do than be as nosy as his mother was often in the window and would see her going past. Spritely-stepped on her way out of the village, and then dragging her feet when she came back. And like the rest of her family who bore testament to the changes in her behaviour, he was intrigued as to what was going on and where she was taking herself every day. But unlike the others, however, Dai, never far from being backwards in coming forwards, decided he would take it one step further and that he would make it his business…

## Chapter 9

The next morning the clouds had lifted and it was bright and breezy as Dai ventured out to look for his friends. He found them kicking a ball up at the playing field at the top end of the village and they watched his approach with mixed feelings. Dai, for the most part was alright, but he could be unpredictable and his recent escalation of feelings for Cerys made them feel slightly uncomfortable. But he had been house-bound with his man-flu so the break from his company had been a welcome one and they greeted him warmly.

"Fancy going in goals, then, Dai?" Twm offered blandly and Neil suppressed a grin. All three of them knew Dai couldn't save a ball to save his life.

"No, never mind that. I was thinking something more... Adventurous."

They raised their eyebrows. That could mean anything from mildly entertaining to downright dangerous with Dai.

"So what have you got in mind, then?" asked Neil, intrigued despite himself. It was the tail end of summer, nothing ever happened around here, and you could always count on Dai to devise some distraction. Both he and Twm were all ears.

"Well, how do you fancy checking out the church? You know, have a scout about, see what's what."

"See what's what?" echoed Twm in puzzlement, "We know what's there. An old knackered church that some mad biddy hung herself outside of and a load of ghosts, allegedly!" he shook his head and glanced at Neil who was staring at Dai with a bemused look on his face.

"This is about that cripple you beat up, isn't it? Do you think he's still there, then, or something! Bloody hell, Dai, let it go, he's probably long gone."

Dai fixed Neil with a steely glare, "Oh has he! And who's to say he hasn't? I left him in a pretty bad way; maybe he's been unable to go *anywhere*!"

"Why do you say that? What's changed? You weren't that bothered the other day. Has someone seen him or something?"

"Not quite," said Dai defensively, "but every day I've seen Cerys..."

"Oh no, not Cerys!" Twm broke in with a chortle, "Oh give it up, Dai, you're never going to win that battle, leave it be, mun."

Now it was Twm's turn to feel the icy glare.

"Shut your mouth! I've seen her passing the house every day on her way... to where? You answer me that! It can only be the church and it can only be to see *him!* Where else would she be going? She's only ever gone for an hour or so and she definitely doesn't go on the bus."

"How do you know that?" enquired Neil mildly

"My mam asked Mrs Jones. She goes to town most days so she would know and I'm telling you now she doesn't take the bus!"

The two friends thought about this for some moments and then looked at each other.

"The man has a point," said Twm, "there's nowhere else, unless she's taking a walk... or something." he finished lamely and lifted his shoulders.

Neil turned to look at Dai, "So you think he's still up there, and that Cerys is still doing her nurse, angel of mercy thing?"

Dai nodded.

"Well there's only one way to find out, then, isn't there!" cried Neil and kicked at the ball. "Come on, Twm, you coming?"

"Of course!" he glanced at Dai who rewarded him with a boyish grin.

"Okay, boys, what we'll do is this. We'll go in very quietly, just in case Cerys is still about, but to be honest, I saw her going before ten this morning and she's usually back within an hour or so and its half eleven now. And if he is still in there..." he paused and his eyes were bright, "you leave him to me. Whatever his game is, I'll be putting a stop to it once and for all..."

To be sure that Cerys still wasn't at the church, Dai got Neil to go and knock for Delyth on the pretext of asking her out on a date.

"Well how's that going to work, then?" said Neil perplexed, "I can hardly ask Del out and then ask if Cerys is in the house, that's going to look well dodgy."

"You'll find a way," breezed Dai clapping him on the back, "Go on then, lover-boy, we'll meet you at the bench."

Neil scowled but did as he was bid. Peeling off from the others he made his way across to Ty Gwyn as the other two assumed a nonchalant air as they strolled out on to the street. They made their way to the far end before the bend in the road brought them out towards the bench up on their right. They sat and waited, saying nothing as the odd car passed the junction, and it wasn't long before Neil came puffing up to meet them.

"I hope you didn't run all the way and draw attention to yourself!" Dai said irritably, "Well, is she in or not?"

Neil caught his breath, "Yes... she's in! Safe and sound."

"How did you manage that, then?" Twm asked, "It's not as though you're her favourite person. I bet she told you to sod off!" he sniggered and Dai smirked.

"No, she didn't actually. I just asked her if she and Cerys would be up for a double date with me and Dai and the rest was easy!" he dodged laughing as Dai cursed and aimed a cuff.

"Del said she'd think about it but that she couldn't speak for Cerys. Called her a moody cow, as well. Bloody hell, there's no love lost between those two, is there?"

Twm chortled, "You're not far wrong there, mate. Okay," he said turning to Dai, "so what happens now?"

"We go in – quietly! No messing about, and when we get to the clearing we spread out. If he is there then he'll probably be in the church, but better to be safe than sorry."

"Bloody hell, Dai, he's just one man! Are you expecting an ambush or something?" quipped Neil, and Dai gave him his best glare.

"No, I bloody don't, but I don't want to catch him outside and then lose him when he spots us. We just need to make sure he's not outside is all!"

"Well he'll have to sprout wings to get away because the last time I saw him he could hardly walk!" said Twm archly, "Unless he's made a miraculous recovery from the pasting you gave him."

Dai glowered. "Well, whatever! Just keep behind me and *stay quiet*! Come on!"

He lowered his bulk into a semi crouch and scooted across the road to the woods. Neil and Twm rolled their eyes and grinned at each other. Whatever happened, just seeing Dai Jenkins go into some kind of commando role was worth tagging along for, and they loped after him taking care to make minimum noise.

As all three came towards the clearing, Dai lifted a hand and made some vague signal that his friends assumed meant they should fan out. They eased themselves around the trees and bushes looking all around but no one else was in sight. From their points around the perimeter they indicated this to Dai who gestured they now come to him and they huddled down together, eyes suddenly bright with anticipation, breath coming in shallow gasps.

*God, but this was better than kicking a ball 'round,* thought Neil, as Twm inwardly speculated what Dai would do to this guy if they found him in the church.

"I'm going to go in alone," whispered Dai, "and if he is in there then I'll bloody well drag him out!"

The two friends glanced at each other and there was relief in the look. Neither had particularly wanted to go *into* the church. Outside, yes. The clearing, no problem, and the woods themselves, fine. But not *into* the church itself. No way! They'd grown up with the stories and were of the opinion that there's never any smoke without fire, but if Dai wanted to play ghost-busting hero, then they were more than happy to step back and let him.

"Just keep an eye out, for God's sake. And if for some reason Cerys turns up, find some way to... I don't know, stall her!"

"A bit late for that, isn't it, butt?" Twm said in a low voice. "She probably already knows it was you who gave him a pounding."

Dai jerked his head impatiently, "It doesn't matter, just do what I say and wait for me here!"

As he went to rise, Neil put a hand out on his arm and stayed him for a moment.

"Dai, you're not really going to do much more than slap this guy around, are you?" his voice was serious and there was a grave look about his face, "I mean, you're not going to do something...*stupid?*

There was a tense moment as Dai eyed him with bemused contempt, and then seeing Twm with the same look of concern, he broke into a wide grin.

"What me? Come on boys, I'm shy Dai who wouldn't hurt a fly! I just want a word, is all! Look, don't worry, all you pair of pussies have to do is divert any unwanted traffic and keep an eye out, alright?"

They nodded, but now that they were here and Dai was on a roll they couldn't help feeling uneasy. There was an eeriness about the place, despite the brightness of the day, and the church itself never looked less than a church as it did in their eyes at that moment.

Dai stood up and looked about. It was only forty feet or so to the church doors and one looked to be slightly ajar, and with no hesitation he strode towards them with his usual determined air. He paused and glanced back to where his friends were waiting in the undergrowth and gave them a wink; whether through a forced act of bravado or because he was so charged up they didn't know, but when they saw him push open both of the doors and disappear inside the speed of the doors as they slammed shut behind him shocked them to the core and they shot to their feet clutching at each other.

"What the–!" gasped Twm, and Neil coming to more quickly pulled him back down with a fierce "Shush!"

"Neil, did you see that! Did you see *that*?!" He put a hand to his mouth and looked about wildly.

"Twm, get a grip!" Neil was feeling no less panicky but there had to be a simple explanation. There had to be! "It was just the doors closing, for Christ's sake!" Twm stared at him in disbelief.

"Just the doors closing? *Just the doors closing!* They all but bloody came off their hinges they slammed so fast! And don't you say any bloody different, Neil Davis, because you know you saw *exactly* what I did!"

His face had become a bleached moon and beads of perspiration pebbled above his lip. Neil wondered if he looked the same. There was also a horrible sickly feeling in his stomach.

"I know, I know," he said in hushed tones, "but maybe it was Dai himself. Maybe he just wanted to add some drama; you know what he's like! Maybe he just wanted to scare us!" But this offering was a poor one and they both knew it.

"So what do we do now?" hissed Twm agitatedly. "And don't ask me to go in there because it isn't happening! What if there's a load of homeless guys holed up in there or something! You know, like friends of the cripple. He must have friends somewhere. Maybe he's called them in! And now they've got Dai! Or what if the stories are true and it's the ghosts!"

Neil grabbed him and gave him a shake, "Stop it! *Stop it!* There's no point in panicking, Twm, he'll probably bounce back out in a minute all full of his usual bullshit. Come on, calm down, butt! We'll just have to wait and see what happens."

"Okay, okay," said Twm, "but how you can stay so calm I don't know, you nearly crapped yourself the same as me!"

The thought of them both defecating in tandem set them off into a giggling fit but it was nervous laughter bordering on hysteria and Neil managed to rein himself in first.

"Seriously though, we've got to ask ourselves what the hell it is we think we're doing... Chasing after some homeless man, staking out an old church, and *allowing...*" he took his eyes off the church long enough to glance at Twm, "ourselves to get involved with Dai and his bloody obsession. And you've got to admit, Twm, he's starting to get a bit bloody scary."

"Scary?" repeated Twm. "More like downright freaky! But yeah, you're right. And if that guy is still about and has rallied a few mates then maybe we should leave him to it."

Neil frowned at him.

"Twm, I know he can be a pain in the arse but he's still a mate, mun, we can hardly *abandon* him!"

"Oh yes, we can!" replied Twm starting to get up, "Sod this butt, I'm out of here! If he wants to play the big man then he can carry on, I don't want it!"

He emitted a loud, 'Ow!' as Neil grabbed him roughly and pulled him back down.

"Don't you dare run off and leave me to it!" he hissed between clenched teeth. "We're mates and we're all in this together, *all of us*! Don't you even *think* about running out on me!"

They stared at each other until Twm reluctantly dropped his eyes first.

"Alright, alright, I'll stick around, but only for you. And whatever's going on in that church with him right now, I don't want to know, and if I hear even so much as a squeak I'm off, I'm telling you!"

"Fair enough," said Neil and breathed out with relief, "and look, if it's any consolation if *I* hear as much as a squeak I'll be out of here faster than you and I'll also be calling the bloody *Heddlu!*"

Twm nodded and they both turned their eyes back to the church doors that remained firmly shut and fell into an uneasy silence. They liked Dai, for the most part, and suffered his self-assumed leadership with ironic humour, but in truth they were as stuck with him as they had been since childhood. For Dafydd Jenkins wasn't the kind of person you turned your back on – in all ways. But he looked out for them and was loyal in his own way, and it would go better for them to be outside and waiting when he finally made his re-appearance.

The minutes ticked by. Twm kept checking his phone for the time but no further conversation was forthcoming and they remained crouched with just the sounds of the woods for company. Just as Neil was starting to get seriously worried they heard a noise from the direction of the church. And with wide eyes and baited breath they waited and watched as slowly, almost ponderously, one of the doors gradually swung open with a deep groan. Twm swallowed with an audible click and Neil's left eye began to twitch furiously as they froze amidst the foliage and somewhere in the woods a magpie cawed loudly like some portent of doom.

And then, just as they didn't think it possible their eyes could grow any bigger, Dai stumbled out from the church and their first thoughts were that he had indeed taken a beating. But as he shambled his way towards them it was soon apparent that there wasn't a mark on him and yet he looked clearly defeated like all the energy had been drained out of him.

They stood up slowly, never taking their eyes from the caricature than had once been the strutting bantam cock of the village. Gone was the confident, almost bullish gait; the aggressive tilt of the chin, the aura of barely-contained menace. Here before them was a very different Dai.

They looked searchingly at his face. What on earth had happened to him? Even his eyes looked empty as though the lights had gone out and the two friends exchanged a frightened look. This was something they were not expecting. A duffed-up Dai. Even a scared Dai, at a push! But certainly not this *shell-like, vacant-looking, shuffling* creature! Neil cleared his throat and made to speak but Dai held out a hand in a 'Don't!' command and pushed past him making his way to the path.

"Hey, Dai! Dai? Hey, Dai, wait up!"

Twm had found his tongue but his voice sounded squeaky. He looked back at the church and saw that the doors were now shut tightly together again and yet he hadn't heard a sound. He turned back to point this out to Neil but he was already scurrying after Dai and like a shot he turned heel and caught up with them.

Dai was moving with a shambling gait but he wasn't talking, and he kept his eyes forward like a man seeking an end to a long and hellish journey. Neil was still trying to engage him but the mouth was a stubborn line and the pale eyes had an odd faraway look. Twm kept glancing behind them in case something was stalking them or worse still, pursuing them through the woods, but there was nothing following and no one in sight, and when they came out and on to the road he had never felt more glad to see the village sign.

Dai stopped abruptly and turned to face them. There was definitely something amiss but he at least was making visual contact with them and it looked as though he was going to speak. They waited expectantly, but with an undercurrent of barely suppressed agitation. They were torn between an urge to detach themselves and an intense need to *know*.

He regarded them intently for a few moments and then in a savage undertone he hissed.

*"Tell anyone about this and I'll kill you!"*

## Chapter 10

As Selinus watched Dafydd Jenkins Junior leave the church with his tail firmly between his legs, she congratulated herself on her handling of what could've been a difficult, if not impossible situation had she not taken this young buck in hand. She smiled at the memory; her punishment, his shocked disbelief, how she'd unmanned him, impertinent pup that he was.

When he'd made his grand entrance, arms braced, jaw jutting, looking for all the world like he'd come in to fight an army, she knew that he had to be contained immediately and was more than willing to oblige.

As the doors had slammed shut behind him he'd jumped with the noise, of course. Sprang around, with his fists held ready, a proper little warrior, all set for battle. But clenched fists had no power here, and neither did the puffed-up prowess of the village bully. An unfortunate-looking and unprepossessing individual, for all the strength of his physique. He was also Llyr's assailant; Selinus knew that, which made him even more interesting.

It was only when he'd spun back around eyes frantically searching the church that he caught sight of her reclining on the altar steps like some lithe, leonine seductress. And his sharp intake of breath pleased her mightily, for Selinus liked to make a bit of an entrance herself, but unlike this buffoon before her she did it with style.

"What's the matter, boy...?" she drawled pleasantly, "Cat got your tongue?"

He made no reply and Selinus gave a light laugh.

"Why Dafydd, you surprise me, you really do! I was under the impression that you *liked* women, indeed that you like them *so* much that you'll fight for them." she raised an eyebrow and he broke out into a cold sweat.

"Indeed, you like them soooo much you'll snoop and you'll sniff and you'll follow like a dog on heat only it's *you* that's on heat, isn't it, Dafydd...?" Her eyes flared dangerously. "Not the *bitch*!"

He recoiled as she all but spat the word at him, but he was rooted to the spot, his mind numbed in confusion, he wanted to shout for the boys but he couldn't find his voice. But he could hear his breath as it whistled through his dry mouth as he gaped at this woman before him. He had never been so lost for words or felt so powerless in his life, and it was a whole new experience for him that left him feeling as helpless as a baby.

Selinus curved her lips at him.

"Oh yes, I know who you are, *what* you are, young man," she took a coil of her silvery hair and began to wind it slowly around her finger, "You're so consumed in your lust that under normal circumstances we would welcome someone like you, and your..." her smile became a smirk, "*appetites!* Such a shame, but everything has its season but that's not to say we won't have a use for someone like you in the future..."

Dai stared at her. What the fuck was she talking about! Who was she? Where was the cripple, and what was she even *doing* here! His mind was slowly reasserting itself but everything else remained static, as though caught in a trap.

"Ahhh..." drawled Sclinus, "I can see anger in your eyes. My, but you are a feisty one, aren't you? But we can't have that, I'm afraid..."

She uncoiled herself from the steps and came sinuously towards him.

Dai took in the odd-looking dress, the mane of tangled hair, the tallness and the slimness of her figure, but it was only when he saw her eyes that he realised he was dealing with something not of this world, and the strength of his anger drained away as did his fledgling courage. And as he gazed horrified, into the two dark pools of black, for the first time in his life he also knew what it was like to feel fear.

There was nothing friendly about this woman-creature who now stood before him and in the moments before she touched him he truly believed that his last hour had come.

With her thin lips curled tightly, she came right up to his face and her scent filled the core of him as the dark pits all but threatened to drown him.

"You must not take this to heart, young man, but," and she grabbed his crotch with such force he thought he'd pass out, "we already have a man for all our requirements. And as much as your... *tenacity* is to be admired, your refusal to step back from the girl called Cerys is not. Therefore, as much as it ails me..."

She leaned into him and began to squeeze. He gasped as an intense molten pain seared through his privates making them swell to unimaginable proportions before they shrank back slowly and settled into a dull, throbbing ache.

It was only with a supreme effort of will that he managed to keep the tears back as the woman-creature cooed, "...You must be taught some manners and know that not all women are for the taking, young man. Great events are being set in motion here and any further interference from you is not to be borne, do you understand what I'm saying... *Dai!*"

She kept him firmly in her grip and he gave a jerky nod, his breath coming in ragged gasps.

"Good. Because if I see you *anywhere* near these woods, or near this church before you are summoned, and believe me, I will *know*! I will render you impotent forever, young man," She put the curling lips to his ear and warned, "Give me cause to deal with you again in this manner...and I will unman you completely, are you listening to me? *Completely...*"

She pulled back and was satisfied to see abject terror coupled with the stupefaction of shock. She released him as quickly as she'd grabbed him and he sagged like he'd taken a massive blow.

"You have no idea what's afoot, and nor is it any of your business."

With hips swaying she returned to the steps and assumed her previous position, "But I will tell you this. You stay away from the girl, boy! You stay away from the girl called Cerys or a full castration will be just the beginning of the agonies I'll visit on you," she cocked her head to one side, her mane shifting, tendrils moving, "I hope I have been clear enough…"

Again Dai gave a jerk of his chin. He felt he could do little else. It was as though he'd been pole axed. But there was no doubt in his mind now that all the stories were true and that this bitch was the woman who'd hung herself outside the doors all those years ago. He didn't know how he knew, he just did. And his mind, struggling to make a room for this knowledge collapsed in on itself and closed down to the bare functioning, and he stood dully like some hapless bovine waiting for the bolt. Selinus waved a hand dismissively.

"Yes, you can go! Oh, and it goes without saying, my young feisty buck, that a word of my presence here to anyone will go ill for you," she gave a wry smile, "Very ill…Now run along, then, and don't forget to take your friends with you, and remember…" she made a snipping motion with her hand, and then opened the doors.

The dramatic change in demeanour as he made his exit, and how the two boys who waited outside would review it, was no small cause for concern and she knew it. It would only be a matter of time before, as dense and as stoic as he appeared to be, a crumbling would set in and he'd talk, which meant things would have to be brought forward. It was unfortunate she was discovered so early, but then it wouldn't do to have some witless village idiot running around spreading panic – certainly not at this stage anyway. But she felt confident she'd mastered and frightened the boy enough to ensure his silence for the next few days at least. And that was all the time she needed.

She gestured into the shadows and the dark souls who had once been lost writhed their way towards her and cowered down waiting.

"Go and fetch the Messiah and bring him here to me!" she commanded.

And like an oily stream of blackness they snaked their way to the altar at speed before disappearing into the gap that would take them down, down…


When Jesus came to Selinus she had risen from the steps and now stood with her head tilted back studying the stained glass window. She turned and gave him a lazy smile.

"Why, the resemblance is quite uncanny. You'd either have to be blind or a fool to say there was much difference, but time will tell and it will soon be upon us, and then will be the real test."

She turned to face him and fixed him with an orange stare.

"We had a visitor here today."

The Messiah raised his eyebrows and looked at her askance.

"Yes," she said, "You may well look surprised. It would appear that the girl called Cerys has him more smitten than we realised, and he dared to come in whilst his cronies stayed outside. And yes, I am speaking of your assailant. Such a reckless boy, and he came determined to do you further harm, I suspect..."

She watched her protégé closely. Although she and her master had been as good as their word and had healed all of his physical hurts, including the mismatched legs and the resultant damage they had caused to his hips, there was still a part of his mind that they hadn't been able to touch. An inner, deeply embedded core of himself that he was strong enough and wilful enough to keep firmly hidden away.

Both she and the master had tried to insinuate themselves past the barriers, of course, but their young Messiah was tougher than he looked, and they could only surmise that he'd made his defences so powerful that only he had access to the inner sanctum and they'd just have to be patient. Nothing is unassailable, her master had said complacently, but he's given us enough for our purpose and the rest will come with time.

It was in this place that he stored all of his deepest hurts that much she knew. But what they didn't know was how reactive he would be if faced with an individual or a situation from his past; and that made him perilously unpredictable.

They had needed more time to soothe, groom and inveigle themselves further into his confidence, but that option was now closed off to them and all because of some village dolt and unrequited love!

A shadow passed across the handsome features and instinctively Selinus knew she was right. There would've been no grace given, no quarter, if their messiah had had the choice, and a brawling, vengeful Jesus would be their ultimate undoing so early in the game. They needed to distract him, keep him sweet, and what better way than along the age-old path of illicit love and liaison. It was high-time things moved to their natural conclusion.

"I have dealt with him, for now. But his coming has meant we must bring matters forward. I speak of the girl and the pending consummation of your relationship. There can be no more delay. It is time."

"Time?" he said.

"Oh Llyr, don't play the innocent with me! You jest, surely? Why, for you to reap what you have sown with the girl, of course!" She leaned into him and slanted her eyes and their depths shimmered hotly, "You'll like it, I promise, and I know you've thought of little else, and why would you not? The girl is like a delicious peach! So come now, don't be shy with me. Let us not play the cajoling game. You have wanted that girl from the moment you saw her and I care not to hear you deny it! The time is right, the girl is ripe, you've eased her fears and drawn her in so deep she's all but panting! Go to it, take her, and cease this nonsense."

Selinus stepped back and he gazed at her in silence. She was perplexed. She had expected some kind of response that would show pleasure, gratitude, or at the very least excitement, but there was nothing. She tilted her head questioningly.

"Why, Llyr, have you nothing to say? You surprise me."

He looked away and she caught something in his eyes that gave her a clue. She brushed his arm gently, her hand rippling across the pristine robes, and she marvelled again at just how *real* he looked, how authentic, even the sudden set of the mouth added to the whole character, and she swelled with pride at their beautiful creation.

Careful to keep her tone neutral and her words light, Selinus knew that the way forward was to coax him if they were to lead him back to the designated path. There were no other roads open to him, despite what he may think, and it wasn't the time – there was no time – to become mulish about contriving the ultimate achievement.

"This is your prize, Llyr, your rightful reward, and this girl wants you so much she is all but consumed by her longing. You are her first love... her *only* love... And how do I know this? Because I, too, was once young and full of love; and freely did I give myself and never have I looked back and wished it different... and she has been loyal, has she not? Loving, attentive, and faithful to her word *and* our cause, unwittingly, I grant you, but she has proven herself to be true and all for the great love she bears you..." she paused and was pleased to see the mouth soften as he considered her words.

"Don't allow past experiences to mar the fulfilment of what lies before you. For to deny yourself this would be churlish and unkind... not least to Cerys. We do not expect *our* Messiah to live the life of a monk. We would give to you and gladly, any girl that took your fancy, but Cerys is as special to us as you are unique. And we will raise her as we've raised you, give to her as we've given to you. And then, when you make your entry into the world and your presence will be announced, she will be beside you, your love, your Cerys, your very own Mary Magdalene."

There was now a dreaminess stealing over his perfect features and she pounced on it slyly and as silently as a huntress of the night.

"And she'll stand beside you when cities fall... and she'll be at your side when nations bow... because *this!"* she took his hands and gripped them fiercely, "is how Nations rise! Empires are built! Kingdoms are made! And how Man has forged his place throughout history by *taking* and *breeding* and *spreading his seed*! We are not offering you this girl to love for love's sake! Open your eyes, boy! What *we* are offering you is the greatest gift there is!"

And as his green eyes became luminescent with growing comprehension Selinus nodded and holding his hands still tighter, cried, "We are offering you the world, my Messiah, the *world*! You are to be the Second Coming! The one who promised to come! The world has been waiting patiently and so it still waits, and *we*, by Satan's breath, are going to give it to them!"

## Chapter 11

Like Cerys, Dai remained tight-lipped about what he'd seen in the church. Despite prompts from his friends, pleas from his mother, and even his father giving him an odd look and muttering something about talking to him when he was ready, Dai refused to speak, or divulge any details of what happened. Always mercurial in his moods, his descent into gruff responses and long silences meant no one could do anything with him, and his friends, in spite of the threats he'd made against them, talked about it constantly between themselves. They were also taking care to stay out of Dai's way, who, thankfully, had gone to ground and they hadn't seen him since that day.

It was Neil who cracked first. Several days later and receiving an unexpected knock at his door one afternoon; he opened it to find Delyth newly made up and looking particularly attractive. She smiled at him brightly, a novelty in itself as glowering around the village seemed to be her usual look, and for some unknown reason he felt ridiculously pleased to see her and invited her in for coffee.

His mother did her usual lip-press when the girl came calling and nodded her head to the garden, an unspoken hint that they have their coffee out there. And, as it was pleasant days, both were happy to pull up chairs on the patio and look out at the fields beyond.

"Go on then," said Neil. "To what do I owe the pleasure, Miss Watkins?"

Del examined an acrylic nail for some moments.

"Well, I got to thinking after your call the other day, and although I know Cerys would rather poke pins in her eyes than be seen *dead* with Dai, I've decided I'm not quite so fussy. So when do you want to go out, and where are you going to take me?"

Neil grinned and took a swig of coffee,

"Well as you put it like that, Del, how could I resist! Where would you like to go? Pizzas in town suit you? Or maybe see a film? Both if you get lucky!"

It felt good to be having an ordinary chat after such an intense few days of whispered conversations and intense speculation, and besides, Neil was never more comfortable than when he was flirting with a girl. He stretched out his legs and gazed at his companion appreciatively, she really was very pretty when she wasn't in the midst of a strop.

"I don't mind," she returned. "Anything! Anywhere! Just so long as it's away from here and Miss Moody Cow! She's driving everyone nuts with her wishy-washy leave-me-be nonsense. Don't know who she thinks she is, but my mam reckons she'd best get her act together if she's starting college in a week or two. Hardly says a thing! Gets right on my nerves, she does."

Neil looked thoughtful. Strange how two people so interconnected and yet not, should be having such a dramatic personality changes. Was there something linking them, he wondered, and if so what was the common theme?

"So where does she go, then, when she takes those walks of hers?" he said casually. "We've all seen her trying to look invisible as she goes back and fore. But where does she actually go to, Del, do you know?"

Delyth tossed her head impatiently.

"Oh Lord knows, she's in and out like a blue-arsed fly! And then when she's not, she's in her room reading *the bible* of all things!" she threw Neil an incredulous look that matched his own.

"I know! I never had her down as the religious type. A goody two-shoes, yes, and soft as a brush, but not someone I'd say was a bible-basher. All a bit weird if you ask me!"

As far as Neil and Twm knew Dai hadn't taken up reading the scriptures, but then what did they know! They hadn't seen him properly since that day in the woods and he still wasn't answering his texts. Neil had called by the day after just to check he was okay and had been sent packing, so who was to say?

"We went to the old church the other day…"

There. It was out. Or at least he had started. Neil hesitated and chewed his bottom lip, "Well, Twm and I didn't, we stayed outside. Dai seemed to think that Cerys was… well, that she had been *seeing* someone there…"

Delyth was intrigued and flapped a hand at him, "Go on, don't stop now!"

"Well, we waited outside because Dai, being Dai *wanted* to go in on his own anyway." He averted his eyes at her amused look and said defensively, "Yeah, well, that place should've been pulled down years ago it's so bloody old! And once you've heard what happened you'll be glad I didn't, because if you've never believed in the stories before then you will now, I'm telling you!"

He could've kicked himself, but it was too late now! Del was hanging on to his every word, her mouth a small 'O' and he thought, ah sod it, and plunged ahead relieved at the unburdening.

"Well, like I said he went in, and I'm telling you, Del, the doors shut behind him so fast I nearly crapped myself. Well both me and Twm, actually, and he was in there a good few minutes before he came out, and I swear to you on my mama's life..." he leaned across, his own eyes big at the retelling, "he *looked* as though he had seen a ghost! Only not one ghost or even two, but like he'd seen a whole bloody *load* of them! He came out of that church, Del, I'm telling you like a man who'd had all the stuffing knocked out of him. And as you know yourself, he's the one usually doing the stuffing, so it was a bit of a shock..."

"So what happened?" Del's eyes were so wide now that the mascara around them made her look like a startled panda.

Neil shook his head, "We don't know. We *still* don't know, and that was *days* ago. He's gone quiet like your Cerys, but only more so. Won't speak to us or text us or anything. Even his mam and dad are worried about him, but he's keeping schtum so we don't know what to think!"

He cradled his cup and with a sheepish air, said, "He did warn us, mind. But that was the only time that he *did* speak! He said that if we breathed a word he'd have us, and to be honest, I think he meant it. He was so weird. And the thing is, of course, is that we don't *know* what happened, so how can we shut up about only half the story, it doesn't make sense!"

They sat in silence for several moments, each with their thoughts. Finally, Delyth spoke.

"Well whatever's going on, maybe it needs to come out. About Cerys and Dai, I mean."

"Aww Del, don't go stirring the pot just to get one over her, please, I'm begging you! I'm going to be in for it enough once Twm knows I've opened my mouth, never mind what Dai will do to me!"

"No, no," said Del, "nothing like that. But I'm concerned, Neil, really I am! And she's my stepsister after all…"

Neil regarded her suspiciously and her blue eyes looked innocently back but he wasn't fooled for one second. His heart dropped like a stone. How could he have been so bloody stupid! She'd just use this to score points and he'd end up getting it in the neck. If Dai didn't break it first! He clutched at the only straw he thought he had.

"Look, Del, getting back to you and me," he said desperately, "if we're going to make a go of things again then I've got to be able to trust you, you know! Trust is really important in a relationship. Please, forget I said anything, it's probably nothing."

"Well unless you lot were high up in the woods, and I know you don't do drugs!" She fixed him with a quizzical look, "Do you?"

"No Del, we bloody well don't, but what I'm saying is—"

*"No!* What you're trying to say is that there's now nothing after telling me there was something! That tells me that there is definitely something going on. And just for the record, since when has a date with cheap pizzas become a relationship?"

As she rose to leave he grabbed her arm,

"What are you going to do? Who are you going to tell?"

"Why her da, of course. He's been worried sick! And all because she's sneaking around the woods meeting some bloke!" she put her mug down on the table.

"Think he has a right to know his precious Cerys isn't so sweet and innocent after all, don't you? Thanks for the coffee."

He watched her leave as his heart sank even further and he thought, *you're losing your touch, Neil!* Ah well, it was too late now and maybe he could deny he'd said anything. He brightened at the prospect. Yes, that was it! If word got out, then he would just flatly deny she'd heard it from him. There had only been the two of them in that conversation and no witnesses, it would be his word against hers. He breathed a sigh of relief and thought it best he calls Twm and put him in the picture though. Just to be on the safe side. Twm would back him. Twm wouldn't leave him at the mercy of Dai's wrath. He was a good mate. They'd figure it out between them.

He stood and picked up the mugs and didn't see the figure next door partially hidden by the shrubs. His neighbour Mrs Jones might be old and tottery on her legs, but there was nothing wrong with her hearing. And no sooner had Twm returned to the house than she, too, went back into hers carrying her small basket of washing.

The small eyes were troubled behind the glasses and the brow more wrinkled than usual. What she'd just overheard disturbed her greatly. And although Mrs Jones wasn't a superstitious old lady, she was a religious one, and there was only one place to go to with a story like this. Putting on her coat she left her cosy cottage and made her way up to the minister's house at the other end.

As Mrs Jones was making her way along the single street, Delyth was relating what Neil had told her to her mother. Catrin, a practical woman, immediately made her daughter promise not to say anything either to Cerys or anyone else. It was for her da to sort out, she told her. He'd be home from work soon, let him deal with it. Aware that Cerys was currently up in her room, pouring over her holy book, no doubt, Delyth thought gleefully that it might just be fun to stick around for when the fireworks went off, so getting herself some snacks and a juice, Delyth settled herself in front of the TV for some afternoon soaps and waited for her stepfather to arrive home.

Cerys meanwhile, far from indulging in bible study, was carefully applying rarely-worn make-up and thinking about what to wear. Indeed, her mind was far from any form of biblical teachings, for her relationship with the Messiah was on the cusp of a new level. A special level. A more *intimate* level. For yesterday he had kissed her. Suddenly he'd bent forward and brushed her lips with his. It was like how she'd imagined an electric shock would feel, such was the sensation that trilled through her. She'd swayed almost swooned and he'd grabbed her, but tenderly, lovingly, and pressed her to him murmuring her name as he stroked her hair. So overwhelming was her fear and delight she thought she would die!

The inner conflict she'd been feeling came spilling out one afternoon as they sat together on the steps. And with great tenderness he had soothed her fears and stroked her burning cheeks saying that she wasn't to be afraid of him, her love for him, nor their feelings, (*their feelings!*) for each other. For, he had a confession of his own, and yes, that was that he felt the same. And that it didn't matter what she, history, religious teachings, or even the world thought he should be – he was *still* a man and a man he would be; in *every way*! How she thrilled to hear him talk this way and in such an assertive manner. His arguments were reasoned and persuasive, and he reminded her that this incarnation would be very different this time around. More *real*, more human, less… restrictive. He was the Son of God after all, and nothing was impossible. Indeed, he made it clear that it was *her* that he wanted, and to be more than just a trusted companion. Much more.

He had then sent her away from him with that thought spinning through her mind, yet the message was unmistakable and her heart felt fit to burst! It just didn't seem possible and yet it was! For it was Him! It was definitely *Him* and she pinched herself all the way home because it was herself who he wanted. *Her!* Above and beyond all others! His heartfelt assurances and words of devotion had wrapped her firmly into a cocoon of befuddled but very genuine belief. And He had spoken. She was His. Just a short time now, not long before everything became clear, he told her. Things were about to happen and happen soon. But first he had to be sure of her commitment to him. Indeed, his father had decided in his wisdom that there was really only one way for Cerys to prove herself worthy, and that was to lie down with his son thus earning her place at his side.

As Cerys applied just the merest hint of rouge, her mind replaying his words and the kiss over and over, the man who would be her lover waited for her in the church, but he didn't wait alone. The woman who was once called Sarah was with him and she was far from pleased. Jesus had a stubborn air about him and was staring at his feet.

"You're taking too long!" she told him. "Why do you need more time? *We haven't got time,* I explained this to you! Don't you dare find a conscience now when we're so close to success! Don't you dare! You must act soon and without further delay! She is coming tonight and you'd best get to it, boy! I am warning you!"

Her eyes were afire with frustrated ire but she was restraining the greater part of her fury for fear of what she would do to him. Llyr's reluctance to complete the seduction of the girl had become a tiresome and unforeseen development and, charged with the task of overcoming this, Selinus was no further on than she'd been two days ago, and the dark Lord was becoming dangerously restive.

"A kiss and a declaration of love is not enough! Why do you persist in this stubbornness? What is wrong with you! You've all but promised the girl and yet you prevaricate! Continue in this vein and you will jeopardize everything that has been put into place, and we are so *close* to the great unveiling, *so* close! And you decide to get cold feet *now?* I don't understand you, Llyr; your reluctance to consummate the union is beyond me!"

Exasperated she glared at the downcast face but he made no comment. How that tiny part of him that stands so strongly could be defeated she wished she knew. But time was running out and they needed his cooperation every much as they did the soul of the girl.

As for Llyr, he knew why he held back, and had he confided his reason to the spitting cat before him, she'd mock and ridicule him and chastise him even more. And a battle raged within him for indeed he wanted Cerys and all of the trappings that had been promised, but it wasn't just lust that drew him to her. It had never really been just that. He had feelings for her that were as alien to him as this creature before him, and although he'd thrown in his lot with the darker forces, there remained in him something still decent and he balked at the taking of something so precious.

He loved her, and too much to commit the final betrayal. He knew what it was like to be used and exploited, how he could sully such loveliness, such purity, when everything was a lie. Yes, he'd gone with it, he'd been coached and coerced with promises and persuasion, but he knew what he was letting himself in for and had been given the choice.

Or had he? Either way, did it matter? Cerys had nothing to go on other than her faith in a false prophet and the innocence of her heart. And for shame, he had allowed her to be drawn in as inexorably as he had, and now caught in a deadly web of deceit it was as though everything bad that had ever been done to him was coming around full circle. Only *he* was the one helping himself to something he had no right to; it was him who cultivator and manipulator; the taker; the abuser, and it repelled him to his core.

As though reading his thoughts Selinus pinned with a fiery eye but her words were cold and brittle with menace.

"Don't play with us, boy, I'm warning you. Don't think you have choices left or scruples to bargain with this late in the day."

She took his chin firmly and made him meet her stare, "We have been nice, we have been kind, we have *more* than fair and we've been *patient*... and whatever dreams or romantic gestures are going on in that pretty head of yours, *cease them now*! No more excuses, no more prevarication, you will take her forthwith, or I'll take her down to the Devil myself and I'll make you stand and watch. Now which one is to be?"

He dropped his gaze and she knew she had won. Releasing her hold she nodded.

"Good. Now, enough of this nonsense! She's on her way and everything is in place so brace yourself and gird those loins and give her a ride she will remember! Hellfire and brimstone, boy, you might even enjoy it!"

She threw back her head and barked her guttural laughter before flitting to the altar and disappearing beneath. The sounds of her mirth echoed with her descent as she hurried to inform the Master that the renegade pup they'd raised so high had well and truly been brought into line!

# Chapter 12

As Bryn Watkins closed the front door behind him his wife met him in the hallway.

"Huw Powell is here," she said and nodded her head towards the front parlour, "I've put him in there to wait for you. He wants a word, Bryn. It's to do with Cerys…"

He looked at her questioningly and she lifted her shoulders.

"He wouldn't say exactly, just something about odd goings on up at the old church, and as Delyth came home with a tale this afternoon almost word for word, she's also had a word with him."

She gave his arm a pat and smiled encouragingly, "Try not to look so worried, bach, maybe it's just been a case of teenage hi-jinks and scare-mongering. You know what youngsters can be like. Here give me your jacket,"

He dipped his head and gave her a quick peck on the cheek. He'd never regretted the day he'd married this woman – even with her nightmare of a daughter to contend with. She would never be a replacement for his first love, Manon, but she was a warm-hearted and practical woman and he derived much comfort from her, as he knew Cerys also did.

"I've just put a pot of tea in with him, and I've given fair warning to Del so you won't be disturbed."

She gave him a little push, "Go on, he's not been waiting long and it's probably nothing to get *pigog* but you do need to hear what he has to say."

And without further ado she turned back to the kitchen calling to Del to come and help her prepare tea.

Mystified Bryn turned the handle and went in. The chief minister of the village chapel stood up and they greeted each other warmly before Bryn gestured they sit down.

"I'm sorry to have kept you waiting, Huw. The traffic was terrible out of Carmarthen. Tea?" He poured for them both and offered the plate of sliced bara brith before settling back and stirring his cup, as he said, "So what brings you here, Huw, Catrin mentioned it has something to do with Cerys?"

Huw Powell was small in stature but memorable for the mass of snowy hair and thick moustache that lent him the nickname 'Moses' amongst the younger children. He was a no-nonsense, plain-speaking man with a reputation for feisty preaching's and had been the head of their church for more years than Bryn could remember. He was also a very good friend.

"I have come, courtesy of some very strange tidings, to be honest, Bryn," the older man said gravely. "I had a visit from Mrs Jones, not an hour since with the most extraordinary tale. She told me she was bringing her washing in when she accidently overheard a conversation between young Neil Davis next door and your Delyth."

The two men exchanged a look. Mrs Jones was the inveterate village gossip and it was common knowledge that anything she came out with was best seasoned with a good amount of salt.

"As a rule, I know that some things that get brought to my attention are worth little more than the air they arrive on, but in this instance," He placed his teacup and saucer carefully down on the small table before him and took a small Welsh cake, "Either Mrs Jones has surpassed herself in the realms of even her imagination, or else what she says is true! And if I'm to be honest, Bryn, the story your Delyth then told me was almost word for word which leads me to believe it could well be! Either way, I'm concerned, Bryn. Deeply concerned."

As Huw Powell proceeded to fill in the details Bryn listened carefully never taking his eyes from his face. When he finished Bryn exclaimed.

"The old church? Do you mean to tell me, Huw, that my Cerys has been meeting someone *there*, and that Dai Jenkins, who we all know is sweet on her and seriously unstable, went there in pursuit of...who? What?"

He frowned perplexed and rubbed a hand across his face, "I'm very confused, I have to say. I've also been at my wits end with her, she's become so secretive but she won't tell me anything! But thinking about it, when she does disappear, it isn't for that long which could tie in with the church, I suppose..."

He gave a heavy sigh.

"Alright, so what are we *really* saying here, Huw? That my girl has been seeing some stranger in the church or else perhaps getting in with a bad crowd? *Duw*, we're talking *Cerys* here, a more level-headed and sensible girl you'd be hard-pressed to find in the county. And yes, before you say anything, of course I'm going to be biased, she's my daughter after all! And so like her mother in that way, I just can't see her sneaking off to meet some boy who she could as easily meet in town... or even here, to be honest. I just don't see where all this is adding up, if I'm honest, Huw."

The old Pastor raised one shaggy eyebrow.

"Daughters have a habit of growing up, my friend, and as soon as they do they also become adept at keeping secrets. Catrin tells me she's been behaving oddly, Bryn, and I'm not just talking about her not being her usual self, but that's she's also recently taken up reading the bible...Cerys? We haven't seen her in chapel for nigh on six years at least. So why the sudden interest? And why had she been crying one day when she came out of the woods..."

He nodded at Bryn's look of alarm, "Mrs Jones saw her. Spoke to her. Said she all but knocked her over she was so...distracted. Cerys reckoned she was missing her mam and was just having a moment, but Mrs Jones seemed to think it was something else, and I don't mind saying that I think I believe her for once!"

Bryn was thoughtful, "When was this?"

"About a week or so ago.

He took a sip of tea then went on, "It is my belief, Bryn, that there is someone, or some persons using the old church for meetings and Lord knows what else. You hear of these cults springing up. Or perhaps, it's just the youngsters messing about and frightening each other. The place has a history, as we all know…"

"Ghost stories told around winter fires to keep the children away, yes, Huw, I remember them well, but that still doesn't explain why Cerys is going up there, unless…"

He stopped and swallowed hard, "I know that young people, especially those who've lost someone sometimes play around with those boards called a… a…" he floundered for the word.

"Ouija," the Pastor said quietly, "Ouija Boards, very controversial and highly dangerous, so I've heard. Yes, the thought also crossed my mind. They could be holding séances up there or something and maybe things have got out of hand. It would certainly seem to be the most likely explanation at this point. Young people tend to be curious about these things."

Bryn sprang from his chair slopping what was left of his tea into the saucer.

"Well, then there's only one sure way to find out! I'm seriously concerned now, Huw, and I want to go up there. Now! Will you come with me?"

"Of course, this concerns us all. But there is also something else you need to know, Bryn; I called by the Jenkins' house before I came here and tried to get Dai to speak to me about what happened with him. The boy was like a clam. I couldn't get a word out of him. And his mam said he's been like that for days. Difficult, she told me, moody and withdrawn." He stood up slowly, "And that's a worry in itself, Bryn, because I never thought I'd see that boy more mouse than man. Not in my lifetime!"

They heard the sound of the front door closing and both looked out as Cerys slipped past the window and Bryn grabbed at the Pastor's arm, "There she goes! Come on, let's hurry, I think she must be going to the church now!"

"Bryn, contain yourself, mun," Huw said calmly, "If she is going to where we think she is, at least let's give her time to arrive. We don't want to be spooking her, now do we? Steady now, one thing at a time."

"Yes, you're right. I just want to know what's going on, is all. I'm seriously worried now, Huw."

To distract himself Bryn leaned back down for his cup and took a gulp. His hand was shaking so much the cup rattled as he placed it back on the saucer. He watched as Huw slowly pulled his coat on and had to suppress the urge to hurry him.

They went into the hall just as Delyth came out of the kitchen.

"She's just gone out! Cerys, I mean." she announced with barely-suppressed excitement in the blue eyes, "so are you going to go after her then, and see what it is she's been up to?"

"Del…" called her mother warningly, "come back here and finish peeling these potatoes or I'll be coming after you!"

As Bryn pulled on a light jacket he said, "Huw and I are just going to take a little walk, Cat."

"Have you got your phone, Bryn? Just in case …" Catrin came into the hall wiping her hands on a tea-towel,

"Phone?"

"Well yes, bach, in case you walk into something and need some assistance."

"Yes, yes, alright!"

Bryn's manner was unusually abrupt as he fumbled in his work coat for is mobile. He had visions of Cerys embroiled in some life-after-death pursuit with other hopefuls, keen to make contact with departed loved ones, beholden in their curiosity and out of their depth. He had a sinking feeling inside and he didn't know why, only that his daughter was in some kind of danger and he needed to get to her *now*!

His hand found the phone and then grabbing the front door he held it open for Huw to pass first, his foot all but tapping with impatience. Catrin, recognising the signs said firmly but in a kind tone.

"Now don't you go rushing in there like a bull at a gate, Bryn. Nice and easy, now."

As they left the house the wind had got up and there was the smell of rain in the air as the afternoon gave way to early evening and they each pulled their collars up against the sudden chill. They didn't say much as they made their way slowly up the street. The Pastor's pace was more of a stately stroll, and Bryn inwardly champed at the bit that he couldn't quicken the pace.

Eventually they came out of the village and then, not fifty yards on their left, was the path that would lead them to the church. Just before they turned on to it, Huw came to a halt and, putting a hand on Bryn's sleeve, he stayed him for a moment.

"It's been some time since I've walked in these woods..." he said quietly, "and even longer since I put my nose in that church. And Lord knows what we are going to find there. But if it has been a case of dabbling in the occult, Bryn, and that, as you know is my best guess, my *only* guess. We must be careful how we deal with it. We'll need to be *sensitive*. Do you understand what I'm saying?"

He gave Bryn a keen look and had a brief nod in return.

"Alright. Then, please, would you be so kind as to let me take your arm as the path is not so even as it once was and I don't want to be taking any unexpected tumbles."

Bryn offered his arm and they proceeded along the path before coming out of the green gloom into the clearing. They stopped at the very edge and took a quick look around their surroundings before turning their gaze to the church.

The doors were firmly shut, but they could see a faint light seeping out from beneath. The two men shared a glance. Someone was definitely in there. As they went to move forward for some inexplicable reason they were both overcome by an overwhelming feeling of paralysis.

"Huw!"

"I know."

They remained frozen in place, bewildered into silence until the old Pastor said between clenched teeth.

"I don't know what's going on here or even why this is happening, but I was born and bred in this very country, as was my da, his da and his da before him! And the day I can't walk abroad in it is the day I'll lay down in my box and willingly! Black magic or the devil's work, I'll not be held back by either. *God give me strength!"*

And with his eyes fixed firmly ahead he pushed against the invisible barrier and reaching out he found Bryn's hand and clasped it firmly, saying.

"Let us pray, brother, and have faith God hears our voice, for there is something here that would keep us from the church and Cerys. Pray, I tell you, like you've never prayed before!"

In low tones they began to pray together as a gentle rain fell upon them and a lone blackbird called its last post into the night. Calmness began to steal over them like a gentle cloak, and the very air seemed to lighten as the feeling of restriction began to fall away and they turned and looked at each other. The old Pastor put out a leg and took a step forward, then another and another. Bryn followed suit and then all too soon they were at the church doors.

Bryn cocked his head against the wood but could hear nothing, and unable to wait a minute longer he pushed against the great slabs of weathered oak and they gave way with an ease that surprised him. And as they opened gradually, smoothly, without even the hint of a rusty hinge, the light rushed to meet him and in the heartbeat of a moment he took in the scene before him and his jaw dropped.

As though from far away he felt Huw's hand alight on his shoulder and heard his quick intake of breath. Their entrance had passed undetected and they stood for several seconds unable to believe what their eyes were telling them.

A host of candles had been lit and they cast a soft, glowing light across the whole of the dais where there sat the altar in the middle like a great hungry mouth. But it wasn't the two jagged slabs of stone that took the two men's' attention; it wasn't even the drapes and the furs, the rugs and rich furnishings, nor was it a table laid for supper with silverware that gleamed and twinkled, or even the bed that lay to the side untumbled but voluptuously inviting; it was the sight of Bryn's daughter caught up in a passionate embrace and by a figure unmistakable in his appearance, so familiar in his bearing, so undoubtedly, undisputedly *him* in his 'look' that at first they just couldn't countenance it.

But it was what he was doing that turned the world on its head for he was *kissing Cerys*! *Kissing* her, like he would eat her all up! And the world tilted even further as they saw her responding as slowly they began to lean down towards the bed.

Huw was the first to speak.

"*Iesu Grist!*" he cried hoarsely, "What in God's name is *this*?"

The two figures sprang apart as though scalded and looked around with shock.

The old Pastor stepped forward several paces emboldened by his fury and threw out his arms,

"What sacrilege! What blasphemy!"

Hearing Huw shouting brought Bryn to his senses and finding something of his voice, he croaked, "Cerys…"

His daughter gave him a look he couldn't decipher before moving closer to Jesus as though she seeking protection. Protection? From him!

Bryn lost his power of speech as quickly as he'd found it. It felt as though all the air had been sucked out of him and he could only stare in befuddled shock, but Huw was still in full cry and furious with it.

"Speak, I tell you! What devilry is this! And in a house of God, no less! Shame on you! Shame on you both!"

The old Pastor was white with rage. Bryn had never seen him so angry but he was thankful for it.

"Cerys, you come away from him immediately and go to your father!"

She hesitated looking mutinous and he roared, "Now!"

Jesus whispered something to her and she peeled herself away from him reluctantly. The three men watched as she retrieved her coat from the floor and pulled it around her, her face sulky with resentment. She looked again to Jesus and he nodded imperceptibly, and slowly with a slight strop in her step Cerys came down from the dais and towards her father.

Bryn felt a surge of relief and finally found his tongue.

"Cerys... what are you thinking of? God, I've been so worried! Are you alright?"

As he pulled her to him she went stiff in his arms and he pulled back looking at her in hurt confusion. His pain was further compounded by her lack of eye contact. Where was his daughter? What on earth had happened to her?!

He turned to the man on the dais, his usually kind features distorted with distress.

"What have you done! What have you done to my daughter? If you've given her drugs, God help me..."

His voice was harsh and fuelled with emotion, and for the first time in his life he felt capable of violence. Huw hearing the imminent threat in his voice, cried, "Bryn! Get her out of here! Don't argue *just do it!* And call the Heddlu!"

The old Pastor kept his eyes on Jesus, and as Cerys was escorted from the church his eyes followed her departure. Their expression was unreadable but Huw could've sworn he glimpsed a strange kind of relief.

"Now then, boyo," he said in a low, angry voice, "do you want to tell me what all this is about!"


As Cerys' father ushered her from the church he was careful to leave the doors open, but he was far from happy leaving Huw to his fate. He was over seventy, for crying out loud, and no match for the young man inside. And although he was the spitting image of the Messiah, it wasn't really him, was it? Or was he?

Bryn's head was a maelstrom of questions but they'd have to wait. First things first. He drew Cerys across to where the path began and she came passively much to his relief. And as he rummaged for his phone his eyes were on her face.

"Did he touch you?"

She shook her head; but still wouldn't look at him. There was a flatness to her gaze, and he had to consider the possibility that she really had been drugged. Why else would she be like this? This wasn't his Cerys. His heart did a flip. *Dear God, no...*

He found his mobile at last, and pulling it, said, "Don't worry, cariad, we'll get this sorted. Once the police get here."

"No!" she cried and with lightning speed she snatched the phone from his hand and flung it into the woods.

"Cerys!" he was almost speechless with shock.

"No! *No* police!"

She pulled out from the crook of his arm and there was sadness in her eyes.

"You don't know what you're doing," she said quietly, "nor do you don't know what you've done."

"*Then what*? What's going on Cerys? You're making no sense! Please tell me what this is all about?"

His voice broke but she regarded his anguish coolly and in a self-assured voice said, "That's Jesus Christ in there that Huw Powell's yelling at, da... *Jesus*! And if you don't fancy seeing him sent down for shouting at the Son of God, then you'd best go in and stop him."

"Wha... What? Cerys, what are you telling me? That... that the man in there *is Jesus?!*"

"Yes, da, I am." she said simply.

Bryn ran a hand through his hair. The storm in his mind had now become a tornado.

He stared at her and now for the first time she looked back him clear-eyed and perfectly composed. Dear God, but she believed it! She really did! But then what if it was true and the man who looked like him, *was him*! He paused to consider the possibility and then discarded it. No, no! This man she *believes* is Jesus practically had his tongue down her throat. No, he would not believe it!

"Cerys, he was *kissing* you!" he said earnestly. "The real Son of God would never do anything like that, never..."

She gave a complacent smile and it chilled his blood.

"That was the *old* Jesus, da. This is the new one. And things will be different this time. *Very* different. And that's because He will be different and because of what's going to happen..." she tailed off, a small frown creasing her brow.

"What's going to happen?" breathed Bryn a knot of dread beginning to form in the pit of his stomach.

"I can't say. But what I will say is that you need to pull Mr Powell out of there before he says anything else he's *really* going to regret. Ah, too late..."

Bryn heard a loud screech and then turning to look he saw the unbelievable sight of Huw Powell as he came tumbling out of the church before landing in a heap. The doors boomed shut behind him and Cerys with a little sigh, said, "I did try to warn you"

## Chapter 13

The walk back up to the village had been agonisingly slow, fraught with tension and unanswered questions. Cerys moved along the path as though in a dream and had withdrawn back into herself after muttering something about her da and Mr Powell ruining everything. Thankfully, Huw had sustained nothing worse than a few bruises but his pride was sorely dented and his outrage continued to burn, but more as a simmering beneath the surface.

When Bryn had gone across to him, still holding on to Cerys with one arm, he was in dread of what he'd find. Broken bones, a fractured skull, but someone or something must've been looking out for old Mr Powell and he'd managed to get to his feet himself after flapping Bryn away.

"The bitch," he breathed hollowly once he'd gotten to his feet, "the bloody bitch t*hrew me out!"*

Bryn was shocked to hear such words come out of the minister's mouth. In all the years he'd known him, he had never known him swear. And as Huw bent over catching his breath with his hands on his knees, Bryn thought to hold on to his questions until they were out of the woods and away from any danger.

"Did you call the police?" said the Pastor eventually between gasps.

Bryn shook his head in agitation; he was deeply shocked at this turn of events.

"No... no, she... Cerys threw my phone! My God, Huw, are you going to be alright?"

"I will be in a minute and don't... worry about calling the Heddlu, Bryn. What we've got going on in there... is no matter... for the police..."

As Bryn went to question him further Huw straightened up with a puff and fixing him with a fierce eye, added, "This is no matter for them, believe me... but first things first, we need to go away from here, and now."

Bryn didn't argue and when they finally reached the road that would lead them back into the village, Huw pulled away from the support of Bryn's arm. The first stars of the night had come out and Bryn looked up at them as though searching for answers; he just didn't know what to think anymore. But his friend and first minister seemingly did. As soon as they reached the gate to his house he said,

"Get your girl under lock and key and then be at the chapel as soon as you can," he winced as he took the step up on to his path adding, "I'll phone 'round the others. We need a meeting and this can't wait."

Bryn nodded to the receding back, and then crossing the road he made for home as Cerys, as pliant as a trusting child, went with him. But he was taking no chances, and as soon as they were in the house he took her upstairs to her room and sat her down on her bed. She looked a sorry sight with her hair damp and tousled, the carefully applied make-up all smeared and smudged but he steeled his heart against any softness. His daughter was seriously deluded or else there was something afoot more powerful than he could ever envisage and now wasn't the time for indulgence.

He removed the key from the lock and held it out. Her eyes followed his movements dully.

"I have to do this, cariad, I'm sorry. But until I find out what's going on you'll need to stay here for your own safety. I hope you understand... Cerys?" She made no reply and he drew a deep breath, "I'll get Catrin to bring you up some supper and we'll have to arrange for some... sanitary arrangements. At least for now."

He felt absolutely awful in himself and as a parent for having to do this, but he was of the same opinion as Huw in that she would almost definitely return to the church. There was obviously more going on in there than met the eye; he just couldn't take the risk.

He took one last look at her wan face and left the room locking the door firmly behind him.

"You must not, under any circumstances, allow her out – even for the bathroom! See if we have a spare bucket or something, just until I get back from this meeting and then we'll decide what it is we need to do."

Catrin bent her head, her mind still racing at the incredible tale Bryn had just laid before her. The details had been sketchy, so keen was he to get across to the chapel and meet with the others, but she'd learned enough to scare her and she was glad she'd sent Del off to visit a friend.

"I'll take her up some stew now, Bryn, but please, don't be too long. I'm really not happy about this…"

"No, neither am I, but needs must, Cat."

He gave her a swift hug before hurrying out of the door and up to the little chapel where it huddled at the top of the street. He was relieved to see there were lights already on and he lifted his face up to the fine drizzle in a bid to cool his fevered thoughts.

He wasn't surprised to see that Huw was already there and surrounded by the three other deacons who made up their congregation. Looking smaller than usual, an angry red bump was starting to colour his right cheek, but the fierce light was still in his eyes and going across to him, Bryn took one of his hands and squeezed it.

"Are you alright, Huw? Are you sure you'll be up for this?"

"Up for what?" interjected Mr Harris with a worried frown, "Maybe we can get on with this meeting now you've turned up, Bryn. I've just had to cancel a meal out and the wife is not happy, I can tell you. Urgent, you said, Huw, couldn't wait. What's going on? And why do you look as though you've had a run-in with one of the Jenkins' boys!"

"Now that everyone's here I will explain. Please, be seated…"

Huw took his usual place beneath the large cross facing them. Again Bryn was struck by how diminutive he was, and yet he had held his ground in the most extraordinary of circumstances. And to then have to suffer the indignity of being bounced out of the church like some roistering drunk, it just didn't bear thinking about! But who did that to him? The Jesus-figure? Or someone else? Bryn, more than anyone else present, wanted some answers.

"I am now about to share with you something so extraordinary that I must ask that you hear me out before passing comment," the Pastor began, "I know all of you are familiar with the old church in the woods, and that the place, having been unused for more years than I can remember is of little interest to anyone, God-fearing or otherwise. However, earlier this evening, Bryn and I had reason to go up there, and well... we had what I can only describe as an 'encounter'..."

"What kind of an encounter?" chipped in Mr Morris, his eyes round behind his spectacles.

"Patience, Eryl!" admonished Mr Thomas. "Let him speak."

Huw bowed his head and went on.

"We'd gone up to there to investigate some goings-on that had been reported back to us by a couple of the youngsters," he tactfully omitted any mention of Mrs Jones and her input at this stage.

He needed to have their support and belief from the onset; he could always fill in the gaps later, "What they had to tell us was of no small concern, and as Bryn's eldest daughter has regularly been visiting the place and, well...for want of better words, has been behaving strangely. So we decided to take a look for ourselves and followed her on one of her, er, forays."

All eyes turned on Bryn for a moment and he nodded.

"We weren't sure what we were going to find, of course. But we'd had the idea that perhaps the youngsters had been playing around with the occult and using the church as some kind of meeting place or something..." he spread his hands apologetically, "Well, that was our thinking. Everyone knows the old stories and curiosity can get the better of us all, especially when you're young."

These words met with shocked faces, and all eyes this time remained glued on Huw as he paused to take a sip of water.

"Well, I could almost wish we had found a bunch of kids doing exactly that, if I'm honest because–" he paused and looked steadily at them all in turn, "–what's in that church is far worse than anything some curious youngster could conjure up!"

Mr Harris leaned forward, "Why, who is it, Huw?"

"*What*, would be more appropriate, Ifor..."

Huw's voice suddenly quavered with emotion and he took a moment to compose himself, his mouth working. Unaccustomed to seeing their minister so obviously distressed the small congregation looked at each other mystified. *It's the shock*, thought Bryn, *it's all catching up with him,* and he felt a stab of remorse for having asked him to accompany him in the first place. He stood up.

"Huw, look, I..."

"No, it's alright!" Huw raised a hand and Bryn slowly lowered himself back down to his seat.

"I must do this, Bryn, don't you see? There was more after you left that only I bore witness to and well..."

He gave a wry smile, "It's been quite a night, I know, but there's no need to bundle me in blankets, I'm tougher than I look."

He turned his attention back to the story.

"We found Bryn's daughter, alright, but she wasn't alone. She was with a man who..." he shook his head still bewildered at the incongruousness of it, "Who was...well, to all intents and purposes was purporting to be *our Saviour!*"

An even more shocked silence met this disclosure and then Mr Morris piped up.

"What? As in Jesus Christ? *Our* Jesus Christ?"

"Yes, Eryl is there any other!" Huw said testily, "And mark me when I tell you he looks the part, oh yes, he looks the part alright, could probably fool his own mother! But he isn't the Messiah, he's a charlatan, a false prophet and thank God we came in time!"

Again Huw gave a small shake of his head and lowered his voice so everyone had to strain forward to hear him.

"We walked in to a scene of what can only be described as... a seduction, and Bryn's daughter was in his arms. There was a bed. And furnishings! The whole of the altar area done up like you wouldn't believe! And I tell you now, as God is my witness, I thought for a moment I must be in my bed and dreaming for surely this could not be! But there it was, and right before our eyes! Such was the shock we could barely believe it!"

"Then why haven't you called the *Heddlu?*" cried Mr Harris, "You mean to say there's a man up there masquerading as the Son of God seducing our womenfolk and you haven't reported it? What are we doing having this meeting? We should be having him arrested!" the others, including Bryn, nodded their agreement and looked askance at the Pastor.

"You still don't get it, do you?" Huw said with sudden anger, and with shaking hands he pulled off his jacket and yanked up his sleeves.

Dark bruises were blooming all along his arms.

"Do you see these?" and then pointing to the bruised swelling on his face, "And *this*! And there are others! Oh yes, all over, and believe me when I say that I couldn't feel less battered and bruised than if I had got unlucky with one of the Jenkins' boys!"

They watched him anxiously; they had never known him so... *animated.* Not even when he was preaching.

"Grabbed at! Manhandled! And then thrown clear, *clear* I tell you, from a House of God and by something that had *no* business being there... *has no business* being there!" he paused and took a breath, dark eyes glaring from beneath the shaggy brows. "And don't you think that if this was a situation that needed the police that I would've called them by now? Because let me tell you this if you think by sending the *Heddlu* in there that they'll find anything then you'll be sadly mistaken. Something has taken over that place that isn't human! Something bad! Something *different,* and it's most definitely *not* of this world!"

"Alright, Huw," murmured Bryn. He'd never seen him so upset.

"But, what, what…" stuttered Mr Morris. He looked to the others and spread his hands in failure at finding the right words.

"So the tales are true, then…"

Huw turned to the speaker. Mr Thomas, thank God! As always a sea of calm in a crisis. The lack of questioning in his tone was like a welcome balm and the old minister was able to gather himself.

"Yes, Cliff, it would appear so. For my part, I have no doubt of it… not now."

"But how do you know? How can you say this for sure?" Mr Harris was obviously struggling, "What? That you were accosted and chased out by *ghosts?*"

"No, Ifor, not ghosts…"

Mr Morris found his voice and leaning forward his whole demeanour bristling with shock, he cried, "Then surely not by Jesus himself!"

Huw glowered at him.

"No, Eryl, I only wish it had been! Gentlemen, I know this is going to be hard to believe, and forgive me for my outburst earlier, but you are going to have to take me at my word now as you have never taken it before. Bryn! Pass me that bible!"

Bryn did as he was bid, thoughts falling over each other in his head. What in God's name was Huw going on about! *It wasn't possible… was it?*

Huw took the thickly-bound book from Bryn and holding it aloft, he placed his other hand on it and in loud, ringing tones he declared.

"In the sight of our Lord God, Jesus Christ, I do most solemnly swear on this most beloved and holy book, that everything I am telling you is the truth, and should I bear false witness may God strike me dead!"

He lowered the bible and in the ensuing silence looked intently around at the grave faces. There were no lingering doubts now, not after that. In a quieter tone he went on,

"When Bryn took his daughter from the church, I was so caught up with this parody of Jesus, *so outraged;* I didn't even see where she came from. But she was fast, so fast, because suddenly there she was, right there in front of me."

He swallowed and reached for more water.

"And she was angry, *very* angry! And I swear by all that's holy I've never seen such a thing, such a... *being* like that before. There was *fire* in her eyes, *real flames*, and brethren, the sight of her struck terror into me..." he shook his head at the memory.

"And I don't mind telling you that I believed my last hour had come, and I said to myself, Huw, you've nothing to lose, boy, so just go for it! And I did, I thought, well if my final hour has come, then let it be with a psalm on my lips and so I started to recite the Lord's Prayer and that just inflamed her more. She hissed and she cursed and that Jesus character did nothing but look on, and then that's when I knew..."

He smiled and it lit up the whole of his face.

"That's when I knew for certain that this *wasn't* the Christ! He was no Messiah! For no Son of God would have stood by in His Father's house and endured the foul blasphemies that were coming out of her mouth! And I felt glad, *glad,* that this man was not the Lord, our God, for I would have rather willingly laid down my life than to have seen him so debased in sin! And then I was afraid no more... It didn't matter whether she struck me down or let me live; I saw the truth of it and knowing this, she cursed some more before picking me up and throwing me out into the night!"

He drew breath and eyed his captive audience. They stared back. He was like some biblical character of old that had wrangled with the devil and lived to tell the tale. And if what he was saying was true, then...

"This is why, my friends, we *cannot* go to the police. We cannot! They may find the man, but I doubt it, and we would look foolish, to say the least."

He nodded at Bryn, "There is also Cerys to think about, and notwithstanding her reputation, she is also not in a good place within herself at this time and we need to protect her. She has been affected by something so powerful it is akin to spiritual sickness and so we must proceed with care."

He spread his hands.

"Gentlemen, we are not dealing with a normal, *earthly* situation here. It is full of dark influences and unknowns; we know that much. But we must act according to the tenets of our faith and place our trust in the *real* Jesus Christ; this is a spiritual matter and so it must be dealt with in the same vein accordingly."

"And how do you propose we do that, Huw?" Bryn asked the question wonderingly as the full implications of what the minister was suggesting began to sink in. Supernatural forces? Here? In their little village?

"More to the point, how do you expect *us* to do it!" quavered Mr Morris, "Good God, mun, we have no experience of anything like *this*!"

"I know, I know, calm yourself, Eryl," said the minister soothingly, "I did not mean *us* in the literal sense, but we cannot stand by whilst the devil's work goes on beneath our noses *and* in a House of God, for shame! There is evil in our midst and as the elders of this parish we have a duty to deal with it."

"This needs to be referred to the Presbytery, and to the highest level, Huw, without delay."

"Yes, Cliff, and so it shall be but first I need your agreement to something that some of you may find difficult to accept... Some years ago I attended a seminar in Lampeter and there was, amongst the speakers, an extraordinary man called Jonas Llewellyn. I say extraordinary because he is more than an ordained minister, and has, for want of a better expression... talents, that he uses in a much specialised kind of way."

"What kind of *specialised way*?" interjected Mr Harris in exasperation, "Huw, you're making no sense!"

"Alright, Ifor, alright," Huw said, his voice placating, "then let me put it like this; we have a situation here that needs specialised help, and there is only one man I know of who can do this. I want to ask that this man be allowed to come here to us, but first it needs to be put to the vote. He may not be available,

Lord knows, I don't know if he's even in the country, he's always so busy, but I want your support on this, I *need* your support! Because once I go to the Presbytery there will be lots of questions and it's important we present our request as one voice. I'm willing to beg if needs be because I'm telling you, I want this man! We *need him!"*

"There's no need to beg, mun, and you're right; there will be many who will be hard pressed to believe this tale." said Cliff Thomas mildly, "But Huw, I've known you all my life and have never known a lie pass your lips, ever. And if you told me now that the devil himself was on the roof, I'd believe you, therefore it goes without saying you have my vote. I say we ask for this Llewellyn because Lord knows we're out of our depth, brethren, and have nothing else. Gentlemen…?"

He lifted his eyebrows and one by one each Deacon raised a hand and said 'aye'. But there was still a look of uncertainty about Ifor Harris and Eryl Morris, and seeing this the minister said solemnly.

"I thank you for listening tonight; for hearing me out and your willingness to share this burden. It has been such a tale as you've never heard before, I know, and I am incredibly grateful for your support. It is my belief that I looked into the eyes of the devil tonight and although we have no idea of what we are up against; I do know this. That if we are to succeed…"

He paused and there were tears in his eyes. All of a sudden he looked very tired and all of his years. He cleared his throat noisily and went on,

"...if we are to succeed, it is imperative we stay strong in our beliefs. And in each other. We have all known each other for almost all of our lives, and we have worshipped and taken counsel together in this very place and for more years than I care to remember. You are, all of you, my spiritual family, my friends, my brethren. And now, we must be brothers-in-arms in the true sense of the word and stand together against something beyond our reckoning. But as long as we place our trust in God and stick together, we may yet come out of this. Thank you for your time, now if you'll excuse me, gentlemen, I have to go home, there's a telephone call I need to make..."

"Huw?" It was Ifor Harris. He stood up, "I'll come with you, if you don't mind. Moral support and all that... Eryl?"

"Aye, I've nothing else planned than a night in front of the tele so why not."

He smiled. It was a shaky one but a brave attempt. He looked to Cliff.

"Well there's no need to ask me, of course I'm coming! Bryn...?"

Before he could reply Huw spoke for him,

"No, he needs to go home tonight. His place is with his family, particularly his daughter. Bryn, you need to keep her safe, you know that, don't you? She has to be kept away from that church at all costs and most importantly away from *him*."

"Yes, Huw, I know. And the good Lord forgive me but I have her under lock and key." Huw nodded "There's no other way... for now."

As the men made preparations to leave Bryn stopped at the door and turned back to where the minister was making slow passage from his seat as the others fussed around him solicitously

"You know," he said quietly "I've not thanked you properly for saving my daughter for indeed it was your actions that in all likelihood saved us all, and for that, I am forever in your debt, Huw... but I also have a question I would ask, if you don't mind?"

"No, go on."

"I didn't see this creature that attacked you, but I did see the man. And I'll be honest with you now and will say that I really, truly believed for a moment that it *was* Jesus I saw in that church and had I been alone..." He shook his head, "I fear the outcome would've been very different... And yet you knew *immediately,* Huw! You knew straight away and yet... how? How did you know for sure...what told you?"

The minister gave a small smile and then making a fist he thumped it to his heart and said simply, "This!"

## Chapter 14

Selinus had turned on the Messiah as soon as she'd cast the recalcitrant minister through the door and her eyes blazed with fury. With a sweep of her arm all of the drapes and the luxurious furnishings disappeared in an instant as though they had never been and he stepped back in sudden apprehension unsure whether he would be next.

"That man! That *minister*! He has ruined everything! *Everything*!" She spat, "Am I to be tormented forever by these God-fearing vermin? We were so close and now we'll never get her back!"

Her narrow chest heaved and the mane of white about her head snapped and unfurled as though charged with electricity. The maelstrom of colours raced through her dress as she paced and snarled like a pent-up beast!

"And what am I to tell the master! He'll not be pleased; he'll bay for blood and *you!*" She spun on her heel and pointed a finger, "will be the first to be sacrificed, *Jesus*! For if you had not delayed as you had we would have your seed in her by now and the next part of the master's plan would've been *well* underway! "

The man called Jesus stepped forward, "All is not lost, surely...? Granted, the girl has been taken, but who's to say she'll stay away..."

He left the suggestion hanging in the air and, like a ravenous beast that has found a scent, Selinus pounced on it.

"What? You mean you believe the girl might come back?"

He bowed his head and she raised her eyebrows, the fires beneath them banked for a moment and they glowed with speculation.

"What makes you so sure... boy?"

"Love," he answered simply, "she loves me, or at least she thinks she does. And because of that, I believe she'll come back..."

Selinus barked and then looked at him in amusement, "Then you'd better be right, hadn't you, or else you're doomed, boy! For we'll visit on you all the agonies and more that were ever afflicted on that man who once rode a donkey into Jerusalem, because *that!*" she narrowed her eyes malevolently, "is what happens to those who thwart the will of the master. Death! In a thousand different ways, and you my beautiful one, will taste all of them! Now, come!"

She clapped her hands together sharply.

"We must not be here should they return. And if your Cerys gives in to the heat in her loins, then by Satan, you'd best be ready or else she'll be going down with you..."

Cerys, oblivious to the threat made against her life and immortal soul, fretted within the confines of her room as she inwardly railed against her father's interference and for the umpteenth time rattled the door knob. She did consider climbing from the window but it was a sheer drop and what good would she be to the Messiah with two broken legs! But she was determined to make her way back to him. She was consumed by a fever of religious awe and earthy love that intoxicated her to her very soul and she could not understand why she was being punished.

Jesus loved her and wanted her for his own, and yet when commanded he had released her to her father. Why? Her mind was in a spin and refused to be stilled, far removed from her earlier serene state, and she replayed, again and again how he'd taken her in his arms, told her not to be afraid, and how he'd laid his lips on hers, at first gently and then urgently with a rising passion as she melted into his embrace as wanton and as willing as any woman enthralled to her lust.

The last week had passed in a haze as the real world had receded and profoundly enmeshed in the fantasy of a new one, Cerys lost the ability to reason. Like an obedient child she had sat and listened absorbed as her future role was spelled out for her, and down to the depths she went. Nothing else mattered to her now than to go back to her Lord and be at his service, to grant his every wish, to be his to command. College was forgotten as if it had never been: her dreams of nursing, her friends, her da, even her own mother. She shivered miserably and realised that if she was ever going to leave this room, then for the first time in her life she would have to be cunning.

Dafydd Jenkins, too, wasn't having a good time of it and his moods had descended into a deep, dark depression. His mother was at her wit's end, but took her lead from Dai Senior whose directive was to let him be and that he'd come out of it in his own time. And so meals were eaten in silence, his usual favourites on TV went unwatched. He simply lolled about drinking endless cups of tea and eating any kind of foodstuffs he could lay his hands on. Communication came in grunts and in his pale blue eyes was an odd, faraway look that sometimes darkened and then his hand would creep down to his crutch and he'd glower fearsomely.

His friends, Neil and Twm, having tried and failed to make contact with text and phone calls came to a more proactive decision that something had to be done; they intended to call on him the following afternoon. They'd bought a few beers and an action film they knew Dai would like. They hoped to break through his miasma of misery, still intrigued as to what he'd seen in the church that day that had disturbed him so badly. Also they missed him. He was, for the most part a bone-head and a bully, but life was dull without Dai Jenkins Junior and they wanted their butty back.

Huw, the old pastor, had made the call, and despite the shocked disbelief in which it was initially received by the Presbytery, the phone then never stopped ringing for the remainder of the night. Word spread swiftly throughout the upper echelons of the church hierarchy as again and again confirmation was asked for and provided. Support from the other chapel members was stoic now that they were all over the shock, and each one stayed with their pastor well into the night taking it in turns to answer the phone and keep the tea flowing. Huw took a quick bath where upon further examination his injuries showed nothing more serious than a flurry of dark bruises, the worst being the one on his face where he'd landed. Once he was in clean clothes and had imbibed a tot of whisky, the world tilted back into some semblance of normality and when he re-joined the others he brought the bottle.

"I think we all could do with a tut of this!" he said with some of his former vigour. And as the others smiled and held out their cups, old Huw, who had never felt such love and affection since his wife had passed away twenty years before, was greatly comforted by their presence and thanked God for them.

As the big old clock ticked away loudly in the corner they went over the events of the evening thoroughly as each man came to terms with the seeming unreality of it all. They spoke of the church and its macabre history, the possibility that perhaps the youngsters had dabbled in the dark arts after all and unleashed something so powerful they were unable to control it. They speculated, suggested, debated and discussed, but there was only really one man Huw insisted, who would know. And in between the phone calls and another round of whisky, prompted by their curiosity he told them what he knew of Jonas Llewellyn.

Raised in Pontypridd, the son of an ex-miner, who received his calling just after all that business with the strikes. His father became very engaged in his new role and went overseas to administer pastoral care. He was particularly active during the famine in Ethiopia and then when he returned home he married and raised a family, Jonas, who was the eldest, then carried on in his father's footsteps and became an ordained minister before he then got the call, allegedly, for something quite different.

This branch of God's work, Huw explained, was not common knowledge in the secular world, nor was it bandied about the laity for the sake of discretion. It is a specialised calling that requires an inner strength beyond the usual dictates of spiritual engagement, and this Jonas has the natural skills apparently and a track record to prove it. Due to the sensitive nature of his work, only a selected audience were invited to hear him speak that day and even then, the information imparted was just a slight insight into the darker side of theology.

But what Huw had heard was enough to impress him in a way he had never felt before, for not only was this man possessed of extraordinary presence and charisma, but he was also well-versed in all doctrines of various denominations and shared his talents throughout. As a result, he was much in demand and travelled extensively around the globe in an advisory role and as a dispenser of his special kind of treatment. The man had exceptional abilities and, it would seem, he had also been well named, Jonas meaning 'chosen'.

"I just pray he will be able to come to us," said Huw, "and if he does, you will never in all your days have seen his like before – nor are you likely to again."

They pressed him on this, but he'd say no more. Wait until we get the call, was all he'd reply. But hope held steady in his eyes which in turn gave them encouragement, and as Eryl Morris filled the kettle for some more tea Ifor Harris unscrewed the top of the whisky bottle.

Bryn, after returning home first checked on Cerys, who was pretending to be asleep before taking his wife into the kitchen and telling her everything. Catrin listened in horrified silence as he began with their encounter at the church; the confrontation, his removal of Cerys before the village pastor was so unceremoniously booted out, finishing up with the meeting at the chapel and Huw's proposed plan of action. She shook her head in bewilderment.

"But Bryn, the devil in that church or not, we can't keep her locked in! She's *eighteen*, for God's sake! She's an adult, and if this gets out you could be arrested for false imprisonment! What are you thinking?!"

"Of keeping my daughter safe, that's what I'm thinking, Cat, and I'll do what it takes!"

He ran a hand through his hair distractedly, "You have no idea what it was like to walk in there and see her all but in bed with Jesus Christ! And he looked as you'd imagine! I mean, I thought it was him! I would've *sworn* it if not for the fact he was about to bed my daughter! I couldn't believe my eyes! My Cerys, caught up in something like *this*! My God, her mam will be turning in her grave!"

Catrin leaned across and grasping his hand squeezed it tightly, "But you got there in time, Bryn, you got there in time. I'm just still trying to process the fact there's a man up there dressed up as Jesus and playing the Don Juan! Are you sure it isn't just the Ouija-board stuff and someone using the situation to take advantage? There are weird groups out there, Bryn, cults and all sorts…"

"No, Cat!" he broke in impatiently, "This isn't kids or cults or even anything of this world! Huw Powell was attacked, I tell you! Attacked! Lifted bodily and flung over thirty feet *out* of the church like a sack of potatoes! Now you tell me what bloody cult would do that? And what's more, he saw his assailant, *he saw her!* She was in his face shouting all kinds of obscenities before she threw him out only that was no ordinary woman! And besides, he swore on the bible, he swore, Cat! And I believe him! *We all believe him!*"

"Alright, alright, calm down. Here, have some more tea," she reached for the pot, "or would you like something a bit stronger? I think there's some brandy in the cupboard left over from Christmas."

Bryn took a deep breath and tried to compose himself.

"No, love, no, but thanks. Look, I'm going to sit up tonight, keep watch. Make sure she doesn't find some way to get out or, God forbid, anything manages to get in! Can you ring Del and get her stay over with a friend? I really think it would be better if she stops out tonight, just until we know where we are…"

He gave his wife an apologetic look, "I can't risk any further antagonism with Cerys at the moment, not tonight. I hope you understand, Cat, but my daughter has to take priority right now and we need to keep a lid on it."

She squeezed his hand again.

"Of course, I'll call her now."

As she went into the other room to use the phone, Bryn rubbed his eyes and was suddenly overcome by a great weariness. In spite of a life-long belief in Christianity and as an active member of their small but lively little chapel, he had never thought he'd bear witness to the work of the devil in such a direct way. It was one thing to read of such evils, see paintings, watch the odd film that would plant images in your head, and yet the reality for him had been a beautiful man attired in white robes you'd associate with distant lands, a man he knew immediately, whom he recognised in an instant, and that even as that man held his daughter in his arms all but ravishing her, Bryn had *believed* it was him! And still now he inwardly struggled with what he saw and what was in his heart.

As he heard Cat's voice talking to Delyth he raised his eyes up to where his only daughter was lying on her bed faking sleep, and he wondered in a moment of unbridled fear whether the man dressed as Jesus was the very devil himself! And his soul wept for the very thought of it.

When Catrin returned to the kitchen she nodded and then, pulling open the fridge, she began preparations for supper as he watched her and thanked God again that he'd had sense to marry this woman.

"Did Cerys eat anything afterwards?"

"No," she replied ladling stew out for the microwave, "But she did drink a little and so we must be happy with that, I suppose. Oh Bryn, I hope she'll be alright! I feel terrible locking her in her room. Here!" She gave him the key, "I know we must do it, but it just all feels so *wrong*!"

"That's because everything is wrong, Catrin. We just have to sit tight and wait until we hear from Huw. He said he'd call as soon as he had word and then…"

At that moment the telephone in the hall rang.

## Chapter 15

The following day was a Saturday and it dawned bright and sunny, a promising respite from all the recent rain, but there was a cool breeze and a different kind of cloud that hung over the village, and by midday everyone who lived within a stone's throw of it knew what, why, where and how, and were soon talking about it over gates and back fences. Pastor Jenkins took the opportunity to send further news of an impromptu meeting that would be held in the chapel later that day. It would've been futile to have tried to stop the gossip, living in such a small place made any expectation of tongues to remain idle impossible. But he did request that recent developments be kept within the confines of the immediate community and for nobody to go into the woods. Thankfully no one needed any persuading of the latter, but the former would be dependent upon good will and for now, the villagers were so taken up with the drama on their door step that Huw Jenkins reckoned they could keep the news secret until teatime at the least.

A special minister was coming, and his pending visit was causing as much excitement as did the news that the stories associated with the old church were true after all.

The word was that the witch had come back to exact revenge and was using 'Jesus' as her bait. The villagers were agog. There hadn't been such high feelings since the sheep-rustling incident a few years ago and people moved plans and made changes to ensure their attendance at the meeting.

Huw saw it all going on from his front window, and despite feeling sore and tender in places, his spirit remained unbroken, for help was on its way and that gave him strength. The phone had continued to ring throughout the morning but the main work had been done, the endless explanations, testimonies, and questions that were still going around in his head, but he had managed some sleep and a call to Bryn Watkins had reassured him that Cerys remained safe and secure in her room. All that remained now was for Jonas Llewellyn to arrive, and glancing at the old ticking clock for the umpteenth time, the pastor wished for time to fly so the hands would read four o'clock.

Whilst everyone was in a state of high dudgeon, Delyth arrived back on the bus mid-morning and, having never seen so many people out talking in the street, her first demand when she slammed the door behind her was what had she missed? Her mam and Bryn were drinking coffee in the kitchen and she was further intrigued to see them both looking so bleary-eyed. Catrin rose to refill the kettle as Bryn brought her up to date and Delyth in her inimitable style demonstrated her usual sisterly concern demanding, "But she's alright, isn't she? I mean, she isn't going to go off on one like that girl in the

Exorcist, is she? Because if anything starts flying 'round the house, I'm telling you now, I'll be out of here!"

For the first time in hours Bryn and Catrin managed to raise smile between them. Typical Del! But her energy was refreshingly familiar as it was free-spirited and Lord knows they needed some normality in the house. They had checked in on Cerys in the morning and managed to persuade her to partake of some toast and coffee, but her demeanour was listless and she barely acknowledged them.

Bryn's heart broke afresh every time he looked at this husk of his daughter, and when he tried to engage with her, Catrin touched his arm and shook her head saying once they were back downstairs.

"Let's wait until this minister has seen her, by the sounds of it he'll know what to do. She's quiet now, we've not heard her pacing for hours. And she's eaten a little so maybe she'll sleep for a while. It's what she needs at the moment, I think, Bryn."

He agreed, albeit reluctantly, and as Delyth now asked a barrage of questions he and Catrin did their best to answer them as reassuringly as they could, but they had nothing with which to measure against for they were as much in the dark as was everyone else in the village, and getting up to put the cups in the sink, Bryn said,

"We'll know more at the meeting. It's at half past four in the chapel. I'll be going with your mother, Del, but you'll have to say here, I'm afraid. We're hoping we won't be too long, and as soon as it's over, Mr Llewellyn will be coming here to see Cerys."

They expected the usual storm that would follow hard on the tail of any request made to Delyth, but she was surprised them with a nod of assent and they looked each other with raised eyebrows. Perhaps the recent chain of events was having an effect and Delyth, selfish by nature and born to rebellion, was finally growing up.

As Jonas Llewellyn alighted from the train, all eyes that hadn't already had the opportunity to ogle when he was on board did so now as he strode from the platform and to the waiting taxi outside.

He folded himself into a black and white cab and after consulting a small piece of paper he then shared the required destination with the gaping driver. They pulled away and were soon heading out of the town and into the green countryside.

Jonas gazed about him in appreciation of the surrounding scenery and wound down his window, all the better to breathe the air. Having not long returned from a conference at the Vatican it felt good to be away from the heat and all the stiff-necked ceremonial, and as the car ate up the miles he consulted the notes he'd taken when he'd received the frantic call.

Frantic calls, especially the ones that came in late at night were no stranger to Jonas Llewellyn. Having not long unpacked and enjoying a fine glass of merlot before bed, the call, when it came in surprised him a little for the fact of its location. Such a quiet, one could even say, untouched, part of West Wales, that at first he thought it was a prank, until he asked a number of security questions, and receiving the required responses, he then listened intently as a high-ranking minister explained the situation and all but begged him to attend as soon as was humanely possible.

Jonas was accustomed to this. His work was a rare calling and even fewer responded to the call. That made him a busy man and demand was frequent. And as the taxi sped through the country lanes he thought it no coincidence that he should be in Wales when he could as easily be in Mexico, Ireland or Brazil when the call came in, and indeed the timing was fortuitous; but then God worked in mysterious ways, and often with Jonas Llewellyn.

The driver made no conversation but his eyes darted to the rear view mirror repeatedly as his passenger looked out with a serene and passive air. Jonas pretended not to notice, he was used to the attention. He'd grown up in the South Wales valleys and had travelled the world where his presence and appearance frequently drew stares as it did the odd comment. But being the subject of such curious scrutiny bemused him more than it caused offence. He was confident in himself, and besides, it added credence to his unique role and he deemed this more of a blessing than a curse.

The taxi had peeled off from the main road and they were entering a village that comprised of little more than a long street. The chapel was at the far end and a small figure was stood at the top of the steps keeping a lookout. As soon as he spotted the taxi he eased himself down to the road, and waited at the kerb with his hands clasped tightly before him like an excited child. He had a nasty bruise on his cheekbone but an unquenchable glow about him. Jonas heaved himself out of the car and liked him immediately, "Pastor Powell, I presume?"

"It is, but please, I insist that you call me, Huw! Thank you *so* much for coming, sir, we are indebted to you!"

Jonas took the proffered hand and gave it a gentle shake, and then turned to retrieve his bag from the car. The driver was openly goggling but remembered to say thank you for the generous tip and as he reluctantly pulled away, Jonas looked up to the skies where dark clouds were now gathering and then to the chapel where almost all of the village awaited his arrival.

"Ready?" he said to his tiny companion.

Huw drew a deep breath and let it out with a big gust.

"Aye, ready as I'll ever be! Please, Mr Llewellyn, follow me…"


Indeed, almost the entire population of the village were waiting inside. The chapel hadn't seen so many people fill its benches in nearly half a century and the atmosphere inside was positively electric. Bryn and Catrin were sat up at the front next to the deacons along with Mr and Mrs Jenkins, with Neil and Twm sat just behind. The two friends had decided that the visit to Dai's could wait until after the meeting and fill him in with the latest developments and, wrapped tightly and well out of sight beneath their feet, was the twelve-pack of beers to help with the telling.

Everyone was chattering, some in English, many in Welsh, and the din of speculative chatter rose to the vaulted ceiling as it filled the room. The pastor came in and made his way up to the front, his gait measured as always but nobody really took any notice. It was only when Jonas stepped up behind him that the noise levels began to decrease as the villagers at the back saw him first and then fell into silence. As he made his way further along, the gabbling grew quieter as he came into their line of vision, and by the time he'd reached the front of the chapel the air was so tight you could've heard a pin drop.

As both men turned to face the congregation, Huw gave a small cough and extending a hand, he said, "Let me introduce Mr Jonas Llewellyn…"

The special minister looked out across a sea of faces and they gazed back at him in shocked awe. Some mouths were gawping. Others caught in mid-speech were grimacing. And one or two had theirs closed but with a prim pursing of the lips for they had never seen the like, and the seconds ticked by as they all took in their first sight of Jonas Llewellyn.

He was tall, well over six and a half feet and as lithe and lean as a beanpole. But it wasn't so much his great height that drew their attention as the fact he was black with intricate studded tattoos on each cheek. He looked fearsome, exotic, almost otherworldly, and they were stunned. Even old Huw who'd seen him previously and knew what to expect had to admit he cut a striking and imposing figure. Darkly handsome and wearing a flowing black cassock, his unusual appearance was further enhanced by a cap of snowy hair neatly cropped and in stark contrast to the rest of him. And yet he looked no older than forty or so, but the face had strong character and the dark eyes were arresting and full of secrets. Around his neck hung a huge wooden cross almost as thick as a man's wrist, and he brushed his fingers against it before surprising them further by addressing them in a strong Welsh accent. Now they were completely bewildered and there was a slight murmuring, for here was something else indeed! Jonas carried on, his voice rich, deep, and commanding.

"My name, as you know, is Jonas Llewellyn, and I have been called here today to deal with a rather unusual situation that has arisen in your village. I appreciate that there will be many among you reluctant to take on board what it is I am about to say; but know that I am an accredited minister with many years' experience of dealing with the darker forces that make up our world, and yes, they do exist and yes, they can do damage, if you let them."

He paused to allow time for his words to sink in. People were as diverse in their beliefs as they were in strong opinions when it came to the occult. And frequently, as Jonas discovered, their belief systems didn't always make allowances for these things, indeed there were many who opposed the notion vigorously. But Jonas wasn't there to preach to the unconverted, such was his schedule there was rarely time to indulge in endless debate and he was making no exception now. His style throughout the clerical world was known to be assertive and direct, giving rise to the accepted view that a man who wrestled regularly with things in the darkness would obviously develop such characteristics.

"For those of you who don't know... your Pastor," he gestured to Huw stood just behind him, "was attacked yesterday evening in a location not far from here. It would appear that his assailant was not your usual kind of culprit, which is why I'm here. And the reason that *you* are all here–" he fixed them all with a stern eye and several shrank back, "–is because Pastor Powell requested that the matter be addressed openly and as a community issue. I have also been given to understand that there are two other individuals who have been affected by these recent events, and I will be seeing them directly after this meeting."

All eyes remained on him. Not even a rustle interrupted the silence.

"The location, as I'm sure you are all aware by now, is a disused church that has not been used in almost a century. But there is a myth associated with it that I believe has its roots in fact, and it is these facts that I'm interested in for they are as important, if not more so than the myth."

He broke off and, softening his features, gave a small smile that was as disarming as it was unexpected. They looked like frightened sheep, his appearance often had that effect, but if he was to get them onside then a little charm wouldn't go amiss.

"And this is where you come in, for I know you'll have heard all the stories in their many variations and your testimonies will be invaluable to me…"

Some audience members began to relax. There were few things more complimentary than basking in approbation, and they all knew the tales, of course, indeed one or two believed they knew all there was to know. A few faces looked around not wanting to be the first to speak until the mood was broken by a voice that called out somewhere from the back.

"So are you like an exorcist, then?"

Jonas looked for the speaker and saw a ruddy-faced woman who was looking slightly rattled, although he wasn't sure why.

"No, not exactly. I'm more like a spiritual trouble-shooter. I deal with situations that don't come under the remit of traditional pastoral care…"

"Then I hope you've brought a load of holy water because you'll need it!"

"Really?" said Jonas, his face was unreadable.

"He'll need more than that!" someone else piped up and there was a nervous ripple of laughter.

Huw Powell stepped forward with a frown as the woman who had first made comment rose up from her seat at the back and cried, "Oh but come on, you've got to be joking! We're living in the twenty first century, for heaven's sake. This will be down to kids, you'll see! High jinks and messing 'round and all because they've got nothing better to do!"

As she sat back down she whispered something to her neighbour and smirked. Bryn stood up and his face was like thunder

"I'll thank you to hold your tongue, Megan Pugh! Because my daughter, not to mention Dai and Jen's youngest boy," he gestured to Mr and Mrs Jenkins who sat looking tense and uncomfortable, "are not here at this meeting because of what's been going on in that church. And it isn't 'high jinks', let me tell you, because I was there and you weren't!"

Suitably chastened Mrs Pugh dipped her head and, turning to Jonas, Bryn said, "I'm sorry about that, Mr Llewellyn. Please go on."

"No problem," said Jonas mildly but before he could continue another voice chipped in, "I'm with you on that, Mr Watkins! There *is* something bad in that church!"

It was Twm. Standing up slowly he looked around and there was a remembered fear shadowed in his eyes.

"We didn't actually *see* anything, but we saw Dai after he came out... and, well, he looked like he'd seen more than just a ghost and he sure scared *us*! And if this... man, sorry, Mr Llewellyn! Mr Llewellyn can find out what's going on, then, we're all up for it... aren't we?"

He gave Neil a poke in the ribs who winced and then rose to his feet looking earnest.

"It is as Twm says, but..." he looked up at Jonas and gave an audible swallow, "I think you *will* need a lot of holy water, and probably more than one bible because whatever it is, it shook our best mate up badly, and nothing shakes Dai... you'd have to meet him to know that..."

There were nods of agreement and Jonas regarded him thoughtfully. Neil, in awe that he'd even dared open his mouth and give advice to this *giant*, sank slowly back down to his seat as Twm hissed in his ear, "Nice one!"

But Jonas didn't appear to be offended or even mind. Removing the massive cross from around his neck and holding it aloft he said, "You see this? One of the most ancient and powerful symbols known to man. Never underestimate the power of faith, nor the means with which you use it, for it is *that* belief that truly arms you in the struggle. Forget your films and the books that says certain things must be like this, or these things have to be like that, for you will only ever really *know* from your own experience! I have been all over the world dealing with undesirable entities. Evil beings that make it their business to prey on the vulnerable and cultivate their weaknesses. And believe me, they stalk the shadows between worlds and are as real and as tangible as you and me. But they are not all-powerful. They are not unbeatable. Although they may, on occasion appear to have taken an upper hand…"

He paused and touched his head briefly, "They are not to be underestimated… they can hide, emulate, *infiltrate,* and bide their time for as long as they choose to remain dormant. But there is evil all around us, and you only have to look out into the world to see that it's busier than it's ever been and so we must not, at our peril, dismiss the existence of such things. And neither do we sit back and think it'll visit someone, someplace else because we choose not to look. Because *that* is how it gets in, *that* is how it works! And just for the record, folks, I have other means at my disposal and rarely use holy water."

No one moved and Jonas, satisfied he'd made his point replaced the massive cross around his neck and looking around, he said, "Okay, now we've got that sorted, I would like to hear from anyone who has had any first-hand experiences that they would be good enough to share with me. But first, talking is very thirsty work and I've come a long way. I'm assuming you have a kettle here?"

Mr Morris stood up, eyes huge behind his spectacles and said, "We have a burco…"

"Good, then that means everyone can have a *panad!*" Jonas replied briskly, and moved to take a seat amidst some of the villagers.

At the mention of the word 'tea' the room came alive. As some bustled out to the tiny kitchen at the back, others pulled out tins and Tupperware containers and began to offer around bara brith, cakes and boiled eggs. Huw smiled at the scene before him as everyone suddenly came together for that one simple thing that meant so much, and as he threw Jonas a grateful look he was rewarded with a flash of white teeth and a wink as someone thrust a tin of Welsh cakes at him.

"Well!" Ifor Harris breathed in his ear, "I've seen some things in my time. But you've certainly set the village alight with this man! He'll be the topic for *years*! You didn't say he was *black*! How can a black man have such a Welsh name and be from Ponty? And what's with those tattoos!"

"I'll tell you another time, Ifor. What's more important is that he's here!"

"Then I hope he's successful, Huw, because if he can't sort out what's happening in that church, what happens then? What will it mean for us?"

"We'll have to cross that bridge when we come to it, I'm afraid. But what I can tell you is this; he has no fear. No fear at all. And that, I believe is the best weapon he'll have for when he comes face to face with that witch!"

He nodded sagely, "God favours him, I hear, and he also has certain... gifts. Although what they are I'm not sure I want to know, but I do wonder about that cross... I don't know what you think, Ifor, but there's something..."

He got no further as old Mrs Jones bore down on them with a determined glint in her eye, and from the periphery of his vision he could see Jonas, now surrounded by eager faces and brightly-coloured biscuit tins.

The meeting went on for another hour and it was a lively session as just about everyone had a story they wanted to tell. Tales of the witch. Stories of strange lights. Reports of disembodied moans and odd feelings just walking through the woods. Huw and Bryn had the most to contribute, and eyes grew rounder still and gasps became louder as they described the fake Jesus, culminating in the terror of Huw's impromptu assault.

The implications of what this act meant were as riveting as they were disturbing. And the evidence was there, in full view on Pastor Powell's face! And amidst the outpourings of fear and shock were also expressions of indignation bordering on anger and, just as feelings were in danger of reaching fever pitch, Jonas brought the room to order by suddenly coming to his feet and everyone fell into a respectful silence.

He raised a hand, "Thank you, everyone, for all your help. The information you have given me is... most vital. But calm is what's needed now. No good will come of getting angry, believe me. That's like leaving the door wide open and frankly, I think that whatever's in that church has taken enough, don't you think? Let's not make it even easier."

He let the thought linger in the air a moment and as the tension receded deep breaths were drawn and feet shuffled self-consciously.

"It is an emotive situation and I understand well your fears and the need to *act*. But that is why I'm here..." His eyes sought those of Bryn's and he held them for a second, "All I want you to do is to *trust* me. Trust me, and allow me to do my job, for any interference will only serve to distract and hinder and besides, this is a clerical matter, not one for the mob..." He paused and swept them all with a grave look.

"Whatever we are dealing with here, whatever waits in that church, is *not* to be underestimated. Do I make myself understood?"

As all the heads bobbed in unison, he added, "Because mark my words, it has to be something pretty powerful to have breached hallowed ground in the way that it has, and this takes dangerous and unpredictable up to a whole new level and not even I know what to expect. Okay, good! Then all that's left is for me to thank you once more for coming, and please, stay away from the church. If the parents can remain behind, deacons and you, of course, Huw. Just a few final words..." As the crowd started to drift towards the door, there was still chatter but solemnly muted; there was so much to take in and several looked back reluctant to peel themselves away.

"When are you going up there, Mr Llewellyn? Will you be going up tonight once you've seen Dai and Cerys?" asked Twm, who was still hovering about with Neil.

"First thing tomorrow," Jonas fixed them with a no-nonsense stare, "Hope you're not getting any silly ideas, boys...?"

"No, Mr Llewellyn," said Twm, "We were going over to see Dai tonight anyway... if that's still alright?"

He turned to Mr and Mrs Jenkins both of whom had the look of people lost in strange landscape. With a vague air they looked up towards Jonas.

"I don't suppose it would matter would it, Rev?" said Mr Jenkins eventually finding his voice. Usually a confident man and as bullish as his son, the customary fire has been well and truly quenched from his belly by this towering, authoritative giant from the Valleys. And he was *black*, for Christ's sake! *Black and with a face full of tattoos!* This was a whole new experience for Dai Jenkins Senior and, used to being the biggest man in the village, finding himself suddenly in a reduced position was a lot for a man such as him to swallow. And it was only because his wife begged him that he was here at all!

"The boys were coming over anyway, but if you think..." he trailed off uncertainly. Here he was asking another man, *and a black man at that* if it was alright to invite guests *into his own house!* And he felt the heat rising in his neck. Jonas, recognising the type, said airily, "It's up to you, Mr Jenkins. I have no problem with that. In fact, my thinking is that as friends of your son they may well prove useful in opening him up, and so if *you're* alright with that...?"

Looking suitably appeased, Dai's father opened his mouth to answer but before he could get a word out Delyth burst in. She stopped dramatically at the sight of Jonas and her jaw flopped comically. Bryn hurried over to her saying, "What! *What?*"

"It's Cerys!" she blurted, eyes still glued to the figure of Jonas. With a great effort she managed to drag her gaze away and looked into the anxious face her stepfather, "She's gone!"

## Chapter 16

Bryn grabbed Delyth by the shoulders and shook her, "What do you mean, she's gone? I trusted you! *We* trusted you! How…"

"Bryn! No! Stop this at once!" Catrin rushed across and pulled him away, "And Delyth stop your wailing and tell us what happened!"

Delyth straightened the sleeves of her hoodie and glared at Bryn indignantly.

"She tricked me! Said she couldn't use the bucket and was desperate to go," she flushed with embarrassment as some of the eyes on her widened slightly and hurried on, "Well that's what she said! And that she'd only be a minute and that she wouldn't tell or anything, and if I did…" she broke off and looked sheepishly at her mother, "I could also have her room when she left for college. And then when I opened the door she came out so fast she knocked me flying and was down the stairs and out of the house before you knew it!"

As a shocked silence met the news, Delyth adopted a defensive stance, adding, "Well how was I to know she'd do that! I mean we are talking *Cerys*, here, and she wouldn't hurt a fly normally, but, look! I've got the bruises to prove it!"

"That won't be necessary, Delyth," said Catrin and gave a pointed look at her husband.

Bryn held out a hand and then let it drop.

"Look, I'm sorry I laid hands on you... I guess I just lost it for a moment. Please forgive me, Del, it'll never happen again, I swear!"

He turned to Jonas and there was desperation written all over his face.

"Mr Llewellyn, she's gone back to the church, I know it! Back to *him!* This can't wait until tomorrow; we have to get my Cerys back now! She's all I have... she's all I have left of..." his lips trembled and a glaze of tears appeared in his eyes.

Jonas strode across to him and placing a hand on his shoulder, bent down so that he was on eye level.

"Mr Watkins, I would no sooner leave your daughter at the mercy of whatever's in that church than I would my own mother, and *she* was the daughter of a witch-doctor!"

As Bryn gazed back at him struck dumb, Jonas gave a knowing nod.

"Oh yes. I have the best of both worlds in me. But rest assured, my friend..." he suddenly broke into a huge smile but there was something almost primeval and deadly in the baring of the teeth, "I know *exactly* how to use it!"

He straightened up and clapped his hands together loudly making everyone who was still present jump.

"Your attention, ladies and gentlemen, please!" he said briskly and they were all aware of the sudden change in him. Gone was the easiness of manner, the relaxed almost urbane air of conviviality when he'd asked questions, eaten cake and drank tea. Now he was *alive*, alert, and palpably brimming with an intensity of purpose. His dark eyes burned like polished jet and an aura of resolve now seemed to swirl around him like an invisible cloak. He looked like some powerful spiritual warrior of old about to do battle and the small crowd regarded him with a renewed sense of awe.

"There is no time to lose; I will be going to the church tonight. Huw, I would like you to accompany me. Will you be up to it?"

The pastor dipped his head.

"And I will take one other; someone who will act as a buffer, in case you come under further attack. And for this I will need someone who can remain steady,"

His eyes alighted on Mr Thomas, "You, sir, have that air about you – can I avail on your services?"

"Gladly!"

"And Bryn. I will need you there in readiness to retrieve your daughter. Are you up to it?"

"I am."

"Good. Then we'd best get underway."

He turned to Dai's parents who were gazing up at him like he'd fallen from the sky, "I'll not be seeing your son directly, as I'm sure you'll understand, but as long as he's home he's safe. Just make sure he stays there. And boys?"

Neil and Twm stepped forward.

"We can come with you if you like…" Neil breathed his eyes huge with excitement, but Jonas shook his head firmly.

"I'm afraid not. We don't know what we're going to find and your time would be better spent with your friend. Just be sure to keep him away from the alcohol."

His eyes flickered to the bags the boys were holding and they nodded.

"Right, then let's make haste. Huw, lead on."

"Mr Llewellyn?" a voice said suddenly. It was Ifor Harris and he looked perplexed, "should we not pray or something before you lead my friends into this… this *venture*? Forgive me, but you must have some prayer or words of protection, surely?"

All eyes turned from him to Jonas as he smiled grimly.

"Sir, I appreciate your concern, but for as long as God is by our side, he will provide all the protection we need. And besides…" his face changed expression as he touched the huge cross that hung around his neck, "protection also comes in many guises. Have faith in your friends as they have shown faith in me. Now, if you'll excuse me."

Everyone stood back as Jonas, Huw, Bryn and Cliff Thomas came out the chapel and down the steps into the street. A blustery wind was blowing and clouds were scudding across the sky with the promise of rain. It was still early evening but the light was fading fast, and the overall greyness seemed to suit the mood as the small party made their way out of the village.

They made an unusual picture; the tall striding figure distinctive with his white hair and dark colour. Old Huw tottering along in his Sunday best, determination evident in every step. Cliff Thomas not much taller but firmer on his feet and exuding, as he always did, a soothing, sensible air. And then Bryn walking along like a man in a dream, his head hung low as though defeat was imminent, and everyone still left at the chapel came out to watch them depart and silently prayed.

Dai Jenkins Junior also saw them making their way along the street and the sight of Jonas Llewellyn was enough to rouse him from his self-induced stupor so that when his parents let themselves in with Neil and Twm in tow, his first question upon greeting was, "What the fuck was that?"

And their response was to break into guffaws of nervous laughter for it was the first sentence he'd uttered in a week and it had given a glimpse of the old Dai and their hearts leaped with hope. The mood shifted up a few gears as Dai Senior clapped his son on the back and said.

"Some bloody preacher from Ponty who thinks he's Obi Wan! Jen, get some bacon and eggs going, would you, I'm starving! And boys, let's be getting those cans open before we do *anything else* because God knows I need a drink after listening to *that* lot!"

As they all gathered around the kitchen table, Dai Junior listened with less listlessness than he'd shown of late as events of the meeting were excitedly unfolded before him. And as they babbled and the bacon sizzled, the beer went down and then the whisky came out and everyone forgot the words of warning as the youngest and most unpredictable son of Mr and Mrs Jenkins found he had quite a thirst.

And as the rest of the party began to relax and ruminate less frequently, Dai found himself going the other way as all of the tension he'd been holding in his belly began to rise and still the whisky went down. And his mind, gradually waking up and becoming more animated by the minute shook itself like a sleepy dog and yawned widely, but it had a mean eye and was in no mood to be petted. And as he and his friends moved into the parlour to watch their new film, he looked beyond the opening credits and could see nothing but the beginnings of a red mist.

Bryn led the way through the woods as each man followed him in silence keeping company only with their innermost thoughts. The wind whispered loudly through the trees as though egging them on, but no birds heralded the end of another day and watched their passing with wary eyes. The air was filled with quietude and a sense of foreboding, and when they finally came into the clearing, Bryn paused and looked back at Jonas and his face worked with a mixture of anticipation and dread.

The tall man stopped and beckoned him back, and as they waited for Huw and Cliff who were a few paces behind, he whispered,

"Fear is what they feed on. All evil loves fear. Don't give it to them, Bryn…"

His words gave comfort to Bryn as much as the meaning frightened him, but he would walk through hell itself if it meant saving his daughter. Once the men were all together, Jonas looked at each one in turn.

"We are about to go into a something that is not of this world. And whatever it is, it has forced its way through and will not wish to go back. It will be hostile and dangerous and it will fight. It is important that you try to stay calm and do as I say and exactly as I say it."

They nodded.

"And no heroics." He glanced at Bryn, "You especially must not be drawn in nor respond off your own back when we get in there; no matter what position we find your daughter in. You must not react and stay close to me at all times. Now give me your word."

Bryn swore.

"Huw, you must stay back near to the doors and Mr Thomas, I want you to stay with him. At the sign of any trouble you get out immediately and you do not come back in. Under *any* circumstances. Are you both clear?"

Both men nodded intently. They looked scared but undaunted and Jonas felt a twinge of concern. Just three ordinary God-fearing folks from a small Welsh village about to enter a world of darkness and demons that would give no quarter to the faint-hearted and he admired their willingness to put their trust in him.

"God is on our side, remember. And know that he has stood with me in some of the darkest places, and never have I been forsaken. He watches over us now, and already he is at work for the veil of evil that would keep us back has been dissipated."

He took up the heavy cross and kissed it, "Keep the spirit strong and follow me."

There was no resistance to move forward this time and the four men walked forward unhindered towards the church as the wind moaned and unseen eyes watched them approach. As they came to the doors Jonas didn't pause and kept moving forward like an unstoppable force. And as he pushed at the doors they gave way before him and without a lessening of pace he walked in as though he owned the place, and waiting for him at the top of the altar steps was the woman once known as Sarah.

She watched his entrance with narrowed eyes and as he came to a halt at the foot of the steps each took the measure of the other. Selinus was the first to speak.

"My, but you're a fine specimen for a moor, aren't you... big, dark, handsome *and* a man of the cloth, no less! How things have changed ... in my day your sort would've been in chains and little else, and yet here you are as bold as brass and all dressed up and ready to do... *what?"* she said mockingly.

Jonas stared back at her seemingly fixated, but his third eye was busy. There was something near the shattered altar, big, veiled and hidden, but definitely there, and another just in front of it and near to the witch. He had a sense they were hiding something, probably the girl and their Messiah. A quick scan beyond revealed moving shadows but they were no threat and as he finally took in the point of forced entry a wave of righteous anger swept over him.

"Dear God, but you are a brazen bitch!" he said with quiet anger.

Selinus was speechless for a moment before bursting into a cacophony of barking laughter. The men accompanying Jonas covered their ears, eyes as wide as saucers as they beheld the spectacle of this surreal creature.

Distracted by their movements she suddenly stopped laughing as she saw Huw and she pointed, her arm whipping out like a striking snake.

"Why I recognise *you!* It is the minister! Come back for more, have you? Well then, please, come a little closer and I promise *I'll finish the job!*" she screeched and her hair flared wildly as she glared balefully down the church at him, "And bring your churchy friend with you for I'll make a meal of him to the hounds as I will this black devil you have brought before me!"

The pastor paled but retained his composure as did Mr Thomas whose only reaction was to blink as he murmured, *Iesu Grist...*

"Enough, witch!" cried Jonas, "Cease your threats! Your argument is with me and I command that you release the girl at once!" Selinus switched her glare to him her eyes now a fierce red.

"What... girl..." she growled menacingly, "There is no girl here, you impudent moor! And if you've any sense beneath that white woolly head of yours you'd leave now and never come back! Oh how I abhor you, you holier-than-thou hypocrites, always poking about, poking and prying, and *casting aspersions!* Now get out and take your church mice with you! Get out, I say!"

They locked gazes. Jonas didn't move.

"I'm warning you..."

"Such is the language you speak now, isn't it, *Sarah*..." returned Jonas, "Warnings, threats, insults, and... promises... *false* promises! Dreams, illusions, lies and deceit... I also hear you have a Messiah. A Messiah for the Devil, no less! And what promises have you made *him*! As many as he's made to the girl? And don't think your lies will convince me. She's here, alright, I feel it just as I feel the rank corruption of your soul, and so give her to me; but you can keep your false prophet."

Her red eyes widened.

"You think to command *me!* You think you can walk in here and make demands as though you are a Messiah yourself! My, but you reach well above your station, *holy man*! But you are no match, let me tell you. Go now, while you still can, for you try my patience."

"As you try mine, but I'm not leaving without the girl. And so which one is hiding her...?"

One hand had reached up to the cross he wore around his neck and fingering it lightly he walked a few steps to the side and looked around her to where the masked shapes stood quietly, invisible to the naked eye.

"What are you doing!" hissed Selinus.

Jonas ignored her and then holding the great rugged cross before him, he began to intone in a powerful cadence, his voice rising and falling, the softness of the Welsh lilt combining with something stronger, more strident.

*"In the name of the Father, the Son, and the Holy Spirit! By the power of almighty God and the power vested in me..."*

"Cease!" screamed Selinus and she swelled and grew scarlet with rage as the men behind Jonas crumpled to their knees in terror, but Jonas stood firm and unflinching in the face of her wrath as his voice grew stronger yet and filled the church with a fire and brimstone all of his own.

*"...In which we trust and have no fear, for in His Name and in His House we'll suffer no trespass, nor shall we bow down before evil, we'll banish the darkness and bring in the light, the light of our Lord so beautifully bright that not even YOU!"*

His hand flashed out, a blur of black sleeve as he pointed to the huge wraiths hidden behind their veils of invisibility, *"Can withstand the truth of it! And so I bid you now to SHOW YOURSELVES!"*

And then suddenly they were there like looming black clouds on the horizon and Selinus cursed angrily She snapped her fingers and they shifted quickly to her side flanking her like two great beasts coming to heel at their mistress. She glared at Llewellyn but his eyes were elsewhere.

Now that the illusion had been broken Jonas had his first glimpse of the mythical Messiah and Bryn's beloved daughter. Cerys looking dishevelled and confused was in the arms of the man, whom, Jonas inwardly conceded was a convincing and astonishing sight. But there was no serenity in the eyes and he clutched at the girl as much as she clutched at him. They both had a frightened and uncertain air about them as though waking from a nightmare and Jonas knew their shock must be great now that the illusion had been well and truly broken.

He extended a long, dark hand.

"Cerys..." he said, and heard Bryn gasp, and sensed rather than saw him about to move forward. Jonas turned swiftly and gave him a fierce frown which stayed him.

"Spare your breath!" sneered Selinus, "She's not going anywhere, I'd kill her first! You may have had some success with that *pert* little trick but your voodoo magic is limited here! I'm surprised you've not come dressed in fur and feathers shaking a big stick much good it would do you! A moor, an infidel no less! Dressed like a priest and preaching words of a dying God? What *are* you going to surprise us with next!"

She cackled derisively as Jonas kept one eye on Cerys and the other two on the three beings before him. The culminating moment was coming and he knew it, and as he removed the chunk of cross from around his neck holding it loosely in one hand, the witch watching his every move saw this and laughed harder.

"Oh why don't you just admit you're out of your depth, *priest!* Your cross won't save you, and nor will your foreign mumbo-jumbo. You may be as a giant in *your* world, but in mine..." she gestured to the two huge henchmen in turn, "Things are much *much* bigger... *Take him!*" she roared, suddenly.

The two great hulks came back to life and lunged towards him; Jonas jumped back and then did something extraordinary. He curled his cross into himself and with a powerful flick of his wrist the cross suddenly became a staff, and he lashed out with it ferociously as his would-be assailants pulled back uncertainly. He held it before him like a sacred club, his whole body braced in tension and ready for action. He heard the doors slam shut and was glad to know that the pastor had heeded him but there was still Bryn behind him and he knew as surely as he saw him in his mind's eye that fear held him fast, but at least he had two less to worry about.

Selinus made a strange whooping sound her eyes now like ice and glittering with malice.

"Oh but you have brought a stick after all! How clever you are! And certainly full of surprises – the things I could do with a man like you! But you'd have to lose the frock, of course. It doesn't sit well in my eyes at the best of times, but even less so on a blackamoor trying to escape the inferiority of his roots... *heathen!*" she spat.

"You think you know everything there is to know, don't you, Sarah! So consumed with conceit you have raised yourself impossibly high as though born to greatness, and yet once you were no more than a simple country wench who could barely scratch your name and tended sheep!" snarled Jonas, "My bloodline goes all the way back to the Queen of Sheba before you were even a spit in the wind, *witch!* And her line came from Shem, son of Noah, and you dare, with your foul and blasphemous lips to call me a *heathen!* And let me tell you something else. You see this cross...?"

He waved its length before her face.

"It's been hewn from the wood of the Thyia tree – that's the Tree of Life to you! And has been blessed by every holy man who has cared to lay hands on it from the Pope to the Dalai Lama, so I'd take a *good* look if I were you, for it'll be the last thing you'll see!"

*"How dare you threaten me!* I'll take your cross and I'll nail your face to it, you misbegotten son of a whore!" Enraged Selinus threw out her arms and slapping at the wraiths screeched, "Get him! *Take him!* What are you waiting for!"

This time the giant wraiths moved faster and all but overwhelmed Jonas who thrashed amidst their darkness like a man possessed. The staff was a blur as it wheeled and struck, but as soon he appeared to beat back one dark assailant, the other would rear up and bear down on him and then suddenly amidst the furious fight the cross went flying and skittered over to land near to the altar, and Bryn could only look on in horror as the hulking black mass then brought Jonas to his knees. Consumed with dread he glanced up at Cerys, but she had turned her face away, her shoulders shuddering and he knew that she wept. The Jesus-man still held her and his embrace was tender unlike the stony expression that marred the perfect face, and as Bryn heard Selinus roar approval he couldn't bear to look and closed his eyes as hope plummeted in his heart.

Then without warning, Bryn saw an explosion of light from behind his lids and his eyes flew open to reveal a wondrous sight! There came another great flash, then another and another and his knees gave way and he sank to the ground as angels as tall and as bright as his mind could conceive burst out of the light unfurling their wings like great silver dragons!

They launched themselves at the melee where Jonas battled for his life. And the heavenly host drew swords that flashed with white fire and began to slash at the creatures, setting them to howling yet still they fought on as Selinus exhorted them on to greater efforts, but they were beginning to falter and Jonas managed to stagger to his feet.

One of the angels peeled off from the attack and came straight for the witch-woman. And Selinus seeing her approach recognised the face and the intent and hastily threw a ring of red fire about her that the angel could not breach.

"You'll not get me!" she screeched, "You can strike *them* down but you won't get me! This fire will burn you, burn you, bitch! And all your pretty feathers!"

Selinus was panting, eyes ablaze with the thrill of the fight as Lorelius hovered before her, steel in her eyes.

"Come out and face me, you evil wretch! Come out and let's settle this once and for all!" she cried, "I have returned in answer to your challenge *and yet you keep yourself from me*? How brave you are, Selinus, how *noble!* Come forth, I challenge you!"

"Such anger *sister*! Such rage! You have returned with full wings, and swords, too, I see. How impressive you all look, how *grand*! But please, let us even up the odds. As you remember I afforded you the privilege the last time we met, and now you're not playing fair which disappoints me greatly, Lorelius – and you call yourself an *angel?* My! How standards are slipping..." Selinus paused and then said, "And so you leave me with no choice than to call up a few more companions of my own now you've reset the game. And then, when you've been pulled down from your lofty height, I will personally attend to those new wings of yours. They look heavy, sister. But rest assured I will be only too happy to lift the burden, indeed I'll look forward to it. But enough of this idle chatter methinks it's time to let the dogs out…"

The witch put her fingers to her mouth and blew. An eerie almost impossibly-pitched whistle pierced the air and almost immediately more shapes began to push up through the mouth of the altar. And then faintly in the distance and far, far below ground came the sound of muffled barking and the angel's eyes widened,

"You have call on the hounds…?"

"I have, madam!" said Selinus smugly. "And more. Much more."

"Defend the breach!" roared Lorelius and peeled off.

With her sword flaming she led five of the Sisters into the attack as the remaining two struck down the henchmen until their black mass dissipated and they were no more. Jonas had managed to pull free and had staggered a few steps away gasping for breath. His robes were torn and bedraggled but his face was alight with determination and within seconds he took in the battle around him and the sight of the warring angels filled him with renewed vigour. They were flashing blurs of brilliant white as their swords seared and divided the dark shapes that poured up from the breach only to be shattered by the light and burnt back to dust. But still the hordes kept coming.

Jonas now had the grave realisation that this was no ordinary encounter or random pursuit into darkness. The darkness was coming to *them!* In all his years of fighting the many faces of evil he had never known such an assault. And as he heard the approaching storm of the baying pack he understood the significance of their summoning and offered a quick prayer. They were all, still so few, and more importantly where was his staff!

Frantically he cast about and then saw it atop the altar steps just beyond the witch in her ring of fire. A few steps away was the man who would be Jesus, and he saw Jonas look to it as did Selinus, and spinning around to her protégé she bawled, "Get it! Pick it up! *Get it*, I tell you!"

He did as he was bid. Disengaging himself from the arms of the girl he lunged forward and grabbed at it as a drowning man would reach for a rope. He stepped back and looked down at the rugged wood made smooth by loving hands and, as he turned it over and around as though in a dream, the screeching from Selinus reached fever-pitch.

"Put it to the flames! *Put it in,* I tell you! Burn it, *damn you!*"

He looked up and his gaze bypassed the witch as she harangued him furiously and his eyes found those of Jonas and they locked. There passed between them something imperceptible but it was enough, and without further of ado Llyr gripped the staff feeling the weight and pulling back his arm he hurled it like a javelin. As it flew over Selinus in her circle of fire she wailed in frustration as Jonas, as fast as a panther, leaped up and caught it. He landed deftly and only just in time as some monstrous shape bore down on him, and he turned fiercely back into the blackness now equally matched.

His movements became fluid and powerful as he truly came into himself and fought in the ancient combat code of Kalari. And as Llyr's eyes turned towards this extraordinary display, so did those of Bryn and his daughter. For Jonas with his build and height had all the deadly grace of a natural fighter and whirling and turning in his black robes, he sliced and dissembled until the huge thing before him flailed and turned to dust.

But Jonas knew he needed to get to Selinus as yet another creature rose up before him and, like the Sisterhood who furiously fought on, Jonas could only stand and defend his ground as more and more black entities broke through the breach as the sounds of the fiendish pack came nearer and nearer.

The angels were struggling to hold their position and were being slowly being pushed back by the sheer force of numbers. And the witch, now confident of victory dispensed with her ring of fire and turned her attentions to Llyr, and as she vented her wrath with promises of dire and painful punishments so immersed was she in the subject of her hate that she didn't see him coming.

The only one who did was Bryn. Still on his knees and transfixed by the turmoil before him, the spell was suddenly broken by a great crash behind him as the doors flew open and in charged Dai Jenkins who barrelled past him at speed with a wild look in his eyes, his face set, arms pumping. He made straight for Selinus and taking the three steps in one great leap he all but flew through the air and with one mighty punch he felled her!

The sheer pitch of her shocked squawk superseded everything, and for the space of a heartbeat everything stopped as she lay on the stone floor, momentarily stunned. Quick as a flash Lorelius was on her, and as her wings flared with fury she raised the great sword as Selinus clawed desperately at the angel's robes. And Dai, overwhelmed by the images he saw before him crumpled down in a dead faint.

Selinus' hands found marble flesh and she scratched and she gouged and the Head Sister swayed and faltered as she tried to maintain her balance as she stood atop her quarry. The great shining sword wavered and plunged uselessly as the witch bucked and thrashed like a wild beast caught in a net. She heaved and she screamed and then suddenly there were red flames all around her as she regained her powers, and as the silvery wings began to smoulder and burn, Lorelius, trapped within and barely able to hold her position, cried, "JONAS!"

"Jonas!" mimicked Selinus, and rocked some more sending the angel's wings deeper into the fire. "How do you like the heat, *Sister!* I warned you not to come back! Now come, don't fight it, things are just getting warmed up!"

She shrieked with demented pleasure as Lorelius, eyes now wide with panic strove to stay out of the blistering flames, but they almost seemed to reach out with greedy fingers and pull her back in. Amidst the smoke and in her moment of despair, Lorelius called out again. And then he was there.

With the speed of God's blessing he was up the steps, over Dai's form and on top of them in the blink of an eye. And before Selinus could utter another sound he spun the staff around in one smooth movement and thrust the shaft into her mouth, saying,

"*You talk too much!*"

And as Selinus writhed and floundered her eyes wide with shock, the ring of fire died around her as did the flames on the wings of Lorelius, and placing one great foot over the witch's throat Jonas said.

"See to the breach. I have her now."

And as Lorelius rushed to assist her sisters, the witch lay pinned and helpless as her powers waned and the tide of lower beings began to slacken, becoming sluggish and disorientated in their attack. The angels continued to strike them down; their swords great sweeping arcs of light and the dark forces crumbled and fell before them. But the hounds, howling and yelping, still came.

Lorelius, her blackened, smoking wings a sorry sight to see but her spirit undiminished, rallied the host and divided them to each end of the broken slab. And as she stood guard over the lessening gap, the Sisters, with concerted effort marking the ethereal faces, pushed and heaved as slowly, and with a great grinding of stone against stone the two pieces started to come back together, and glancing across at Jonas, Lorelius cried, *"Finish it!"*

Jonas looked down at the wretched creature that had once been human. Who had once dreamed dreams and held high hopes before allowing the darker side of her nature to consume her completely. And in a voice that was almost pleasant, he said, "As I was saying ... about this cross..."

Unable to speak, Selinus glared balefully up at him, her eyes black, opaque, and filled with hate, but she could still hear the pack in full cry and all but at the breach, and if just the tiniest gap remained ... there was final heavy thud as the two parts came together and with it the sound of her doom.

Pretending not to notice Jonas went on conversationally, "Well, it's more than just a cross, you see. It is, as you have seen, a *very special* weapon. Wrought by the hands of my 'infidel' family back in Africa, and made more powerful yet by the hand of God. And so you see, Selinus, nothing is ever quite what it seems ... but there is one thing you can be sure of. I promised you that it would be the last thing you'd see, and I am a man who likes to keep his word."

He leaned down to her distorted face and felt her waves of contempt wash over him.

"There was never going to be a welcome for you in *these* hillsides, witch... *now back to the darkness you go!"*

And with that he thrust the end deeper into her mouth and she gagged horribly as her eyes turned white and her hair shivered and sizzled and began to shrink. The constant race of colours in her dress slowed and became dulled and unmoving, and as the ice melted from her eyes forever, Jonas found himself looking into an ordinary face that some might say was beautiful and honey-brown eyes that had such a look of tragedy he knew he would take it to the grave. But there was no room for pity for trickery was the last card, the *final c*ard this creature could play and Jonas was no fool. Straightening up, he hardened his heart and raising his other arm, he spread out his hand and called out in an ancient tongue that few ears would hear and fewer still understand.

And instantly the whole church lit up as an amazing ray of golden light beamed down through the stained glass window and into his outstretched hand. Like a cascade of molten gold, it carried on through his body surging into the arm holding the staff and then down to the woman who was once called Sarah. And as her eyes widened further and flared for the last time, the light exploded within her and with a small cry she crumbled like paper and then was no more.

The light went out as suddenly as it came in and the silence that followed was broken only by the wind as it soughed mournfully beneath the eaves. And then Jonas turned slowly to face Jesus.

## Chapter 17

As Jonas moved as though to go towards him Lorelius glided forward and intercepted him. Even with her charred and smoking wings she still commanded absolute authority and as he turned his gaze respectfully upon the smooth and lovely face, she said, "A moment, if you please, Jonas."

Everyone watched in wonder as she spread her blackened wings and then shook them briskly. A shimmer of light began to ripple out from her shoulders and it meandered and grew before bursting into rivers of silvery fire that swept through the damaged wings restoring them to their former glory. And after flexing them several times she left them semi-unfurled and the Holy Sisters as one let out a small sigh.

Turning her attention back to Jonas, Lorelius gestured he come closer and rose slightly as she bent her head to his ear. And as he listened intently, his dark eyes were on the false Messiah, and when the angel had finished she drifted back down and moved back to stand with the Sisters.

The tall man was thoughtful for a few moments, as though coming to a decision, then he beckoned Llyr forward.

"Come. Step forward, young man, and give an account of yourself."

His voice was clipped but not unkind as Llyr came out of the shadows and stood quietly before him. Jonas studied him, this man of average height with his wavy brown hair and neatly-shaped beard. The luminous green eyes lustrous and so beautiful that even Jonas had to concede he would've been a powerful and dangerous weapon in a world so easily drawn in by illusion, but there could only ever be one true Messiah, and blasphemy such as was had to be addressed, and sternly.

"Well? What have you to say for yourself?"

Everyone had Llyr in their eye as they waited for him to speak. The angels as they stood over the altar, Bryn, still on his knees as though in permanent supplication; Cerys, frozen in fear half-hidden in the shadows. Huw and Cliff, near the doors where they'd crept back in after Dai's dramatic entrance. Neil and Twm were also there, having followed Dai in his headlong flight, fuelled by beer-based Dutch courage. And now as all four clustered at the back speechless at the breath-taking sequence of events, Dai Jenkins was still out cold on the floor, but no one was in any hurry to rouse him. Llyr dropped his gaze to his sandals and shrugged his shoulders within the pristine robes.

"Nothing," he said. "At least none that would justify what I have done. But for what it's worth, I'm sorry…"

He glanced over at Cerys with a profound sadness and returned his eyes to the floor.

"Your willingness to be used could be construed in many ways, and yet you were at your lowest ebb when you succumbed to temptation and wickedness. Your reluctance to collaborate further in the corruption of Cerys was of particular note, as was the duress under which you then acted. And so what stopped you, Llyr?"

*"You know my name…?"*

Jonas allowed himself a small smile. "Angels know everything." he said simply, "Well…?"

Llyr dropped his green gaze once more his cheeks then blooming with faint colour.

"She'd been very kind to me…" he said falteringly, "…I …I'm not used to people being so nice, and well… it just didn't seem right. Not after all she'd done…"

"Including protecting you from the fists of 'Rambo', here?" said Jonas, indicating Dai's prone form.

"Yes."

"God knows your heart and the trials you've had to suffer, Llyr, therefore, He's willing to be magnanimous and wipe the celestial slate clean…" Jonas paused.

Everyone waited.

"Llyr," Jonas's voice was gentle, "look at me."

The young man raised his head.

"There was a moment back there when you had to make a choice. The easiest one was right there before you, but you took what seemed to be the lesser one and it was in that moment that you truly redeemed yourself. And why? Because you looked at me and saw a man who was *different*, a man who had known trials and injustice just as you have done, and yet had risen above them, *refused* to give them power, and you knew then in your heart that it was not impossible and that it was only *you* who had the right to fulfil your destiny *not* anyone else! And so it was in that deciding moment that you made your choice..."

Jonas nodded and Llyr kept his eyes on his face.

"And it was the right choice. You have been through much, young man. And what evils have been wrought upon you need to be dealt with, but in a better way, the *proper way*, and so what has been proposed is this; that you willingly accompany me up to a little-known retreat in Mid Wales for healing. *Proper* healing! I'm talking as much about the damage you have sustained spiritually as well as in the physical sense."

He gestured to Llyr's lower body, "I'm afraid that we will have to remove the illusory evil that did this. But I can promise you that you'll receive the best care and that your infirmity will be looked at as a matter of... discretion. What is more important is that you receive pastoral care and the necessary healing processes in which to cleanse you."

He smiled suddenly and it was like the sun coming out.

"So what do you say...? Are you up for it?"

A tear beaded the corner of one emerald eye as the young man who had never really wanted to be Jesus gave a tremulous smile and said with quiet humour.

"Anything to get out of these sandals, Father, my feet are killing me..."

Jonas looked at him in surprise for a moment before emitting a deep, throaty laugh that rumbled all the way up from his belly, and leaning forward he gave him a light clap on the back saying, "I can see that you and I are going to get along. I take it that's a yes, then!"

He then turned and looked down the church to Huw and Mr Thomas indicated that they join them. The two men walked as in a daze up to the steps hardly taking their eyes off the angels and then in a kind of stunned wonder at Llyr as they saw him up close.

"Gentlemen, please do not believe your eyes for this young man's name is Llyr! I would be grateful if you could escort him outside and wait for me there, this won't take long. And lads?" He called out to Neil and Twm, "Your friend is stirring, perhaps you could help him outside where the fresh air may revive him better…"

Dai was making groaning noises and trying to sit up, and his friends rushed forward to help him each hooking an arm around their necks and began to walk him from the church. They were almost glad to making an exit, so overwhelmed had they been by the scenario they had just witnessed, and neither boy looked back as Dai's head lolled as he staggered between them. Huw and Mr Thomas followed suit with Llyr between them their eyes glued to him for despite knowing the truth his appearance remained compelling.

The tall man now turned his attention to Cerys who had been watching everything with a mixture of wonder and regret. Her eyes also followed Llyr as he left the church and as Jonas beckoned her forward and she approached cautiously, casting anxious look to her father who drank her in the sight of her like she was an oasis in the desert.

"So Cerys," said Jonas mildly, "at last we meet. Bryn, I think you have made homage enough, come up here and join your daughter!"

Bryn rose awkwardly and hobbled up the stairs, his face a picture of grief and angst, and once he reached the top he held out his arms to Cerys who fell into them with a small sob. He gazed up at Jonas and then to the angels and back again.

"Thank you," he said simply, and then to Cerys, "let me look at you, cariad. Are you alright?"

Cerys allowed herself to be eased out of his embrace and dashing the tears from her eyes, said, "Da, I'm so sorry for all I put you through, but I believed him. I really did! He told me he was Jesus and that he'd come to save the world!"

With a hint of her former self she said, "Trust me to fall for that one, and I'm not even religious!"

Realising what she'd just said a look of mortification came over her face and she turned to face the row of angels.

"Until now..." she breathed reverently, and felt a thrill of joy as each one gave her a small smile and rippled their wings.

There were no swords of flashing fire about them now; each one stood tall and beautifully serene, peace all around them like a nimbus of silvery light. Cerys turned to her father, her face lit with childlike wonder, all tears forgotten as she said, "There really are angels... they really do exist! And Mam is up with them, you know, he told me that..." she trailed off in realisation of what she was saying and a shadow passed over her face, and her voice became hard, angry even.

"Oh how he has tricked me! What sort of a person would tell lies like that? And how *twp* was I to have believed any of it! Oh da, I have been such a fool!"

She buried her head back into his arms and then felt a touch as light as a feather on her shoulder and lifting her head slowly she turned and saw the angel Lorelius before her.

"Cerys."

Her voice was so softly sweet Cerys forgot to breathe. And she was so beautiful, so incredibly beautiful! Cerys was enraptured as she gazed at this perfect being, and when she smiled Cerys would've sworn her heart had stopped beating.

"Not everything you were led to believe was untrue. Your mother is with us. Look..."

And then amazingly, miraculously, the angel's face began to shift and oscillate and then there looking out and in a glow of such love was her mam! Cerys drew breath as did her father and they gazed transfixed until Lorelius' features morphed back into focus and still smiling she gave a small nod before stepping back.

Father and daughter then looked at each other and shared an intense moment of happy *knowing*, and when Jonas then spoke, they both turned to him their faces swathed with euphoric delight.

"Cerys, never be afraid to love, nor lose your kindness and the gift of trust. There will always be people out there wanting to steal the magic, but never forget that it is only yours to give, and so guard your heart, but not so well that the light goes out..." he smiled and then looked to Bryn.

"You have showed great fortitude in the face of such things tonight, I know you fear you will never forget it. But believe me now when I tell you that the others outside will already be having hazy recollections, and by the time everyone wakes in the morning it will all seem like a dream – and so it will also be for those who came to the chapel tonight."

"But why?" Bryn asked slightly bewildered.

"Why, my friend, everyone, including God must have their secrets, or else where is the mystery?" replied Jonas lightly. And with a courteous sweep of his arm, he added, "You may want to wait outside with the others. There is some final business I need to take care of and then we'll be on our way."

Bryn nodded. It was time to go. He guided Cerys down the steps and down the church towards the open doors. The light was fading and suddenly they both felt a strong urge to be outside where the wind was calling and one brave little bird trilled its last song into the night.

As the doors closed behind them Jonas turned to Lorelius.

"My thanks to you and the Sisters. And a question, if I may...?"

She dipped her head gracefully.

"How did this happen? How was she able to break through into such a place of sanctuary? I just don't get it, Lorelius..."

"That's two questions, but I'll answer both," said Lorelius, "Selinus was correct in her assertion that certain powers of evil had been allowed to assemble, and unchecked. We had, many of us I'm afraid, become complacent and careless in our vigil, and that gave wider passage to those who had become powerful in their own right. The witch is only one, there are, and there will be others. And so in recognition of this our Father, in His wisdom, has made some necessary adjustments…"

She flared the great wings out suddenly and they flashed silver fire and then into her hands appeared the mighty sword that hummed and shone brightly with powerful intent.

"Henceforth, every angel shall be armed and winged thus, for evil is all around us, Jonas. Hiding, watching, waiting for its chance. But often we do not see it, and sometimes it isn't even so much of a threat as misguided energy that has lost its way…"

She looked at him pointedly.

"Has the witch so affected your powers, then? Or are they so lost in the shadows that you cannot feel them?"

Jonas, who had many dealings with angels in his line of work, knew that it was not an idle question and that he had missed something. Lorelius went on.

"In truth, it could be said that it was their actions that was the capitulating force for much, if not all that has happened, and this they know, to their great and everlasting sorrow," and raising her voice she suddenly cried out, *"You can come out now! I know that you are there!"*

Jonas felt rather than saw movement behind him, and as he turned around a creeping mass of darkness crawled towards the altar and he looked askance to the angel who then sheathed her sword and folded her wings before saying, "These are the lost souls. Condemned to purgatory for the persecution of an innocent woman and bound to this church for all time. The creature Selinus tried to release them from this state but fortunately for them, she was only partially successful in her endeavours."

"Partially successful...?"

"Yes," said Lorelius, "she was able to exert only a certain amount of influence for a limited time before they couldn't respond to her orders and so became useless to her. Their placement is dictated by God himself, only he can decide their fate."

"And so what happens to them now?" asked Jonas eyeing the mass. Lorelius gave a signal and the Sisterhood moved forward.

"Despite their willingness to rise up and drive the servants of God out of his own dwelling, our Father has shown great mercy and already forgiveness has been granted. He has also decreed in his infinite love and wisdom that they have suffered enough, and so would take them to his Kingdom and show them the error of their ways; but in a *different* way..."

Jonas then looked on in disbelief as each Sister reached into the mewling mass and gently extracted a soul that clung to their robes fervently. And then, one by one as they began to ascend slowly in a gentle swirl each soul held safely in the protection of their wings, a shimmer of gold light appeared and one by one the angels disappeared into it leaving behind one last soul who writhed pitifully before Lorelius. She bent down and scooped it up tenderly and for a fleeting moment before the wings drew around, Jonas caught sight of a young tragic face and knew it to be the minister's daughter. Marvelling at this turn of events, and the unprecedented significance of it he looked at Lorelius wonderingly.

"Just one more question…"

"Then make it swift, Jonas, he is waiting."

"Why?" He said simply.

She smiled and slowly began to turn. A beautiful sphere of scintillating silver as she rose, gracefully like an ascending star up into the light.

"The world is changing, Jonas, and we have to change with it. The Devil has become bold, and so we must adapt if we are to overcome the dark forces he sends against us. But we can still show love, and better to allow love to show the way than remain forever in darkness; for as long as there is light, there is hope, and where there is hope, love will always find a way…"

# Afterword

The little old church still sits quietly in the woods, but walk along the path that'll take you to the outskirts of the village and you might bump into Neil and Twm who'll offer you a guided tour – for a small fee, of course! But their recollections are sketchy at best, and attempts to fill in the gaps meet with barely-concealed contempt as people take in the old musty interior and cracked stained glass window and demand their money back. Even the altar doesn't support their story; just a great slab of stone that rests solidly with not so much as the tiniest crack.

The portal has been well and truly sealed, but the angels are still there. They guard the hallowed ground as they have always done; only their watch is more vigilant now and their swords stay close to hand. As Twm and Neil pursue their enterprise they look down indulgently and at times suppress a smile. For what the two friends lack in perfect recall they make up for in enthusiasm. And they'll be sure to tell you how Dai Jenkins floored a witch with a single kick before taking on the hordes of hell single-handedly, and how they, having had no real choice in the matter then had to pitch in; because you've got to help a mate out, haven't you? And invariably the recipient of this wondrous tale will turn away with a smirk as the angels shake their golden heads.

Dai Jenkins Junior, unfortunately for them, is no longer around to support their story having moved away to play prop for a club near Cardiff. And by all accounts he's doing so well the word is out that he's possibly been earmarked for the Welsh squad. His star is riding high, and he's also dating one of the barmaids from the clubhouse who can match him pint for pint. He's never been happier and is looking forward to a successful career on the pitch.

Cerys has also left the village and is busy studying for her nursing degree making a new life and lots of new friends along the way. Her encounter with the man she thought was the real Messiah has faded away to little more than a bad dream and she doesn't dwell on it; some things are best left in the past and for her, the future, too, looks promising.

Her da and Catrin keep the home's fires burning and it's become a peaceful place since Del, as soon as she turned eighteen, surprised everyone with the announcement she was leaving to work as a chalet girl with a friend in Switzerland. Knowing better than to stop her, her mother and Bryn ensured everything was above board before driving her to the airport themselves and waving her off.

Old Huw, the pastor, prays more than he's ever done for some reason, and has extended chats with Cliff Thomas over the odd tot of whisky. They've formed quite a bond, although neither are really sure why, but they talk about God and religion a lot; whether the world is losing its handle and where it will all take them. They never seem to reach a firm conclusion but both enjoy the process and take comfort in each other's company.

Jonas Llewellyn remains a busy man. The last I heard he was somewhere in America, but no one knows his true movements for sure. He has a way of blending out of peoples' memories once his work is done, which is surprising for a man so striking, but God, as he so often says himself, works in mysterious ways. But he does come back to Wales occasionally and has been spotted in Ponty market with his long black robes and distinctive white hair, the wooden cross heavy around his neck. And, if you're really lucky, you'll also get a glimpse of his much smaller companion who now travels with him everywhere. He walks with a slight limp and has the most memorable green eyes. People often tell him he looks like Jesus Christ, but he just shrugs and laughs it off.

And the village itself goes on about its business and the tales of a witch called Sarah are still regaled around the fires at night. But there's another one about the time the Devil came to call and how their small, seemingly insignificant little village nearly became the catalyst for Armageddon.

But it's just an old wives' tales as these stories often are... isn't it...?

*Bara Brith* – Welsh tea bread
*Bechod* – Pity
*Bore da-* Good morning
*Butt/Butty* – Welsh slang for friend or a sandwich (South Wales)
*Cariad* – Love
*Cwtch* – Cuddle
*Diolch* – Thanks
*Duw* – God
*Heddlu* – Police
*Iechyd da* – Cheers/ Good health
*Iesu Grist* – Jesus Christ
*Panad* – Cuppa
*Pert* – Pretty
*Twp* – Stupid